A mood of harmony settled over them

Dare's lips curved into a hint of a smile, and his blue eyes danced as he sketched. A few moments later he showed Stephanie the page.

The sketch was of a butterfly, its wings spread. But the body and head resembled hers. "To a little bug that grew into a beautiful butterfly, my apologies," Stephanie read. Almost shyly she lifted her eyes to his.

"You're a butterfly, Stephanie," he murmured, his mouth hovering above hers. "An exotic, fascinating creature, sipping delight and giving pleasure from man to man. And I'm just as susceptible as your other men...."

Agonized by his words, Stephanie pulled away. "Your apology is an insult!"

"Who are you trying to impress?" he mocked. "I'm not some callow youth in love with you."

For Ever and a Day

Rosalie Henaghan

Harlequin Books

TORONTO • NEW YORK • LONDON
AMSTERDAM • PARIS • SYDNEY • HAMBURG
STOCKHOLM • ATHENS • TOKYO • MILAN

Original hardcover edition published in 1983
by Mills & Boon Limited

ISBN 0-373-02621-8

Harlequin Romance first edition May 1984

CHAPTER ONE

THE roar of a vacuum cleaner was joined in concert by a muffled soprano. As the top note was reached the shrill insistence of a telephone peal broke in.

'Bother, another few minutes and I would have finished,' muttered the singer. She kicked her long legs and wriggling inelegantly, slid out from under a bed. Her slim hand, clutching the cleaner nozzle like a baton, flicked the roar into a defeated hiss. Hurriedly she ran to the telephone, automatically pulling off a headscarf which revealed a braided coronet of gleaming brown hair.

Her voice was warm with a chuckle as she lifted the receiver. 'Mrs Mopp Services, vacuuming free, singing extra!' The twinkle in the brown eyes deepened.

'Stephanie, is that you, dear?'

The girl smiled as she recognised the slightly puzzled voice.

'Sorry, Mum. It's just the cleaning of my flat getting to me! It's such a lovely day and I was just thinking of home at the farm.'

'It's a wonderful day! I'm so excited, I can't wait to tell you the news! You'll never guess what's happened.'

Stephanie Fernley broke into another wide smile at her mother's words.

'Let me see, you've won the lottery! No? Then it must be the garden prize?'

'No, no! I can't keep it secret any longer,' Mrs Fernley burst out. 'Dare's back!'

'Dare's back?' echoed Stephanie hollowly.

The laughter and happiness in her voice had vanished. Her face, a moment before glowing and vibrant, became a sickly, ashen colour. Weakly she sat down, stricken by the news. She could not speak, but her hand held the receiver, hearing her mother's ecstatic happiness bubble through the instrument. Mrs Fernley, blissfully unaware of the impact her news had held for her only daughter, continued, 'Isn't it lovely? I knew you'd be thrilled. We were having breakfast this morning and your brother Alan let out an almighty yell and ran out of the door as though he was jet-propelled. Then your father saw Dare crossing the paddock and the next moment he was off! I wondered what on earth was going on, then your Aunt Olivia rang to tell me Dare was on his way over from next door. He arrived the night before, completely out of the blue! What a surprise!'

'What a surprise,' Stephanie repeated. Her lack of enthusiasm was not noticed by her mother.

'I just couldn't believe it when he walked in a moment later. Oh, Stephanie, it's so good to see him back again. Of course, he's changed, looks a lot older; well, four years is a long time. Let me see, he's thirty-one now. Still that mop of black hair and those bright blue eyes. He was always such a handsome little boy. Do you remember . . .'

Stephanie found her mind drifting to her own memories of Dare Nayton. He was their neighbour's only son and the only other child apart from her brother Alan for several miles. Alan and Dare had grown up together, and when Stephanie had arrived seven years later, both little boys had been enraptured. The three were surprisingly close, considering, or perhaps because of, the difference in their ages. It wasn't until Dare went to Lincoln to study farm management that Stephanie's feelings underwent a change. She realised that she did not like any of the pretty girls whom Dare took out, although she could tease her big brother about his girl-friends.

The knowledge made her study herself in the mirror with considerable anxiety. At sixteen her long legs and long skinny arms made her look as shapely as an elongated worm, she decided. Her face always looked lively enough, she conceded, but the beauty magazines at the time featured exotic, sultry-looking females. Despite raiding her mother's make-up she could not persuade her upturned, curving lips to look seductive and luscious; they always turned into a grin, no matter how assiduously she practised in the mirror. She had been forced to concede that freckles across her nose and bright ginger brown eyes had something to do with the failure. As for her wide cheekbones, they completely refused to follow the articles' suggestions. Despair had set in and been cruelly emphasised when Dare had popped in with his current lady—a girl who looked as if she had stepped off the cover of the latest magazine.

Stephanie sighed as her mother's voice brought her back to the present.

'Stephanie, isn't that marvellous? We're all so thrilled!'

'I can imagine,' murmured Stephanie.

'And Dare's home for good. He says he'll fly overseas if necessary for his art work. It sounds as if he must have been highly successful. You always encouraged him, you were his favourite model when you were children.'

'There wasn't a great deal of choice,' muttered Stephanie. Her eyes went to a picture on the wall. It was a delicate watercolour, the soft subtle colours highlighting her amber-brown eyes and the soft flowing hair, but not disguising the thin protruding arms and long skinny legs. All the same, she had to admit the picture had a great deal of charm.

'Of course, he was always brilliant the way he could catch a moment in time,' sighed her mother. 'I remember some of the sketches he did of the sheep, and really they were so lifelike.'

'Yes,' said Stephanie, adding silently, I was on a par with the sheep and the horses when it came to modelling for Dare. Yet he had never suggested to any other girl that she model for him. At least, she amended silently, not as far as she had known.

'I just had to ring you to tell you the news. I imagine you'll be ready to down cleaners and drive home immediately to see Dare!'

Stephanie stilled at her mother's words. She felt sudden panic at the thought of meeting Dare again after so long. She knew she could not avoid seeing him now he was home, but surely she could have a few days to steel herself to the idea.

'Stephanie, Stephanie? Oh, I must have been cut off.'

'Sorry, Mum, I was thinking. You see, I wasn't planning on being at home this weekend and I've made a start on the cleaning.' She seized wildly on the first excuse she could find, as her eyes lit on the cleaner on the floor. Realising her mother would think that a very poor reason, she remembered with relief her date for that evening.

'Actually, I want everything to be just right. I've got a

uper man taking me out tonight. Don's from Timaru, Mum, so it would be too late to ring and try to stop him coming through. It's a hundred miles to my flat here in Christchurch, so he'd be on his way. We're going to a party, one of the technicians at work is getting engaged.' Relief made her voice warm. 'It should be great fun. They're a well matched couple.'

'Oh, what a shame! I'll tell Dare how disappointed you are. He'll understand, of course. That reminds me, I forgot to ask him about girl-friends. I wonder if he still has dozens—perhaps he's met someone he wants to settle down with, maybe that's why he's come home.'

The thought of Dare with someone else still hurt, Stephanie discovered. She was glad her mother could not see her reactions. She was obviously over the moon that her 'other son' had returned.

'Well, you'll have to come home after work one night to see Dare. You work so hard, I'm sure you could take an hour or two off. Here's your father home from bringing in a mob of sheep. I'll have to go and put lunch on. Goodbye, darling.'

Weakly Stephanie said goodbye and replaced the receiver. She walked over to the bed and sat on it, her thoughts scattering in several directions, like leaves in a gust of wind.

She remembered the first time Dare had kissed her, the tenderness of his glance and the gentleness of his touch. Like a frightened bird, quivering with emotions, she had returned his kiss, then they had both been dazzled by the passions which had exploded between them. It had been so incredibly beautiful, their relationship, secure in their mutual respect for each other, yet each almost afraid of the power of their feelings. It seemed as if they had only to see one another to be instantly warmed by the contact, their eyes flashing messages of love.

Incredibly, they had managed to keep their love secret. Dare had been working on the farm and Stephanie was already working as a trainee announcer at the local radio in Christchurch. Both knew their parents would be delighted at such a match, yet neither wished to face additional pressure, Dare stating soberly that he had no intention of marrying until he could provide a home. Stephanie felt a tear trickle down her eyelids and run down her cheek. She rubbed it away, remembering her proposal to hire a tent, explaining to Dare that they could get married, go overseas and work their way around the art galleries of Europe, and Dare's practical realism. When the job offer in Wellington arose she had applied for it. Separated from Dare it had been disastrously easy for the break to happen.

The clatter of the vacuum cleaner hose falling to the floor snapped her out of her painful reverie.

'That's enough of thinking about Dare Nayton,' she spoke aloud. 'The last episode in our romantic serial was heard four years ago, and there will be no repeat performance. Our heroine was a young infatuated girl, in love with love, our hero was torn between his desire for her and his desire to paint!'

Her tone was ironic. Despite that, her clear enunciation showed just why she had so easily obtained work as an announcer. She made a mocking self grimace.

'Our heroine is over that first tender love affair. Currently, Miss Stephanie Fernley of Radio Three WS spends her time preparing documentaries and interviews for her own programme, News and Views. And,' she added darkly, 'Dare Nayton can jump ship on the moon for all I care, so there!'

The childish catch phrase made her feel a great deal better. Pulling on her Mrs Mopp scarf, she seized the vacuum cleaner and once again the roar filled the room. But this time there was no singing.

By the time she had finished her cleaning efforts, Stephanie had worked herself into a better frame of mind. Reasoning that she had always known that one day Dare would return, she found herself wondering about him. She wondered if he was just as considerate, and just as quick-tempered, as he had always been. Her mother had said that he was just as handsome as ever, she remembered. Realising, she deliberately thought about her escort for that evening.

Stephanie had met Don twice before, through work, and she had noted his charm immediately. He was in her office when the news of the engagement party had been announced and he had been quick to state that he would be in town that weekend. His readiness to be her partner for the occasion had made Stephanie know a lift to her heart. Don was the type of man to appreciate a care in dressing, and she had a superbly cut green silk dress to wear.

Later, as she added the gold clip to the smooth loop of her hair she had swept up over one side and down into a pleat, she smiled at her appearance. For a moment she wondered what Dare would say. Her face sobered again, then once more she determinedly thrust the thought away.

The voice of one of her fellow announcers spoke softly

from her bedside transistor, reminding her of the time. She tidied her dressing table and turned off the radio as she walked out into her lounge. The room was large and comfortable, with a big old-fashioned chintz-covered suite that had seen better days. One long wall was bare and to relieve that she had placed a large vase of flowers against it.

The doorbell rang and Stephanie smiled. She appreciated punctuality, her work having drilled into her the importance of time.

'Doll, you look beautiful!' Don's eyes smiled into hers as he swept her a mock courtly bow. His blond hair was carefully styled and his clothes chosen to blend with each other. Stephanie stifled the thought that she herself had been selected as a suitable complement to Don's fair good looks.

'I hoped you'd be wearing green or brown,' he confessed as he plucked an imaginary thread from his jacket. 'I'd love to kiss you, but I know how long you would have spent on your face.'

Stephanie resisted the impulse to giggle. She knew Don had meant it as a compliment, but it had made her sound as if she had needed to spend hours.

'Sorry, that didn't come out quite right, did it?' Don laughed easily. 'I'm so used to women protesting, "I've just put on my face".' His clever mimicry made Stephanie laugh. 'Where's the party, doll? I want to show off the most beautiful woman there.' He dropped his voice to a low murmur and held out his arms. 'Although we could have an even better party right here, doll, and really get to know each other better.' Seeing her expression, he smiled. 'But if we must go to the party, let's go!'

Stephanie relaxed once they were at the party. She had many friends there. Don was all attention as Stephanie introduced him to a number of the guests. Her own best friends, Ray and his wife Mat, were among the first, and Stephanie was quick to notice that Don did not immediately query Mat's unusual name. Mat had flatted with Stephanie in Wellington and she knew her friend's opinion of men who made jokes about floor mats or doormats. In Mat's opinion it was nearly as bad as calling her Matilda! They chatted easily together and Don and Ray went to get drinks, Mat's a lemonade as she was pregnant.

'He's charming!' commented Mat, once the men had turned away. 'Where did you find him?'

'Cheeky! He found me. Actually he came in with a new product and was fixing up some advertising and we met then. Last time he was through he heard about the party and agreed to accompany me. He's from your home town, Timaru.'

'I don't know him, though when I heard the name I thought it sounded familiar.' Mat frowned and Stephanie begged her to sit down.

'No, I can't recall, possibly later!'

Ray returned with a lemonade and Don swept Stephanie into a dance. Don was a good dancer, she noted. The local group who were playing were crashing out a strong rhythm and she felt pleasure as her feet followed the fast pace. Her eyes glimpsed Don's expression and she felt pleased that he was so obviously enjoying himself. When the number was over Don led her back rather breathlessly to rejoin their group. The merriment continued and Stephanie had to admit that Don knew every little gesture to charm. He was attentive, and after several dances Stephanie found his company even more pleasing, almost banishing entirely the thought of Dare's arrival home.

'Stephanie, Ray and I are slipping away early. Pop round to see us if you feel like it tomorrow. Bring Don if you like.'

'Thanks, Mat, I'll keep it in mind,' Stephanie promised.

The music changed and Stephanie curled herself into Don's arms. The slow dreamy number made her drift in perfect time, and Don's voice whispering endearments in her ear seemed all part of the magic of sweet romance. She was all the more surprised when she became aware of a group who had just entered from the other room and felt that she was being stared at by someone. It was a horrid, prickly sensation, and instinctively she pulled away from Don's tender touch. A glance at the figure by the door shattered her romantic haze. Stephanie felt her steps falter to a stop and her body become like a lump of lead. Her mouth would not respond to her brain's instruction to give a cool word of greeting. Tremors seemed to charge through her, so she gripped Don's arm for comfort.

The tall, black-haired man met her gaze quietly. He leaned against the door-jamb as though he had been watching her for hours, evidently quite undismayed by her presence. Only the chill of the blue ice in his gaze made his feelings sharply clear.

'Stephanie, Don!' The words were an acknowledgement only.

Stephanie heard Don return his greeting. 'Dare Nayton! What are you doing here? I thought you were in Europe studying old masters.'

He held a hand out, but Dare moved so that Don was left discomfited. Stephanie felt Dare's eyes for a fraction of a second before he turned to Don again.

'There are past masters here,' he said smoothly.

Stephanie saw Don wriggle. Beside Dare he seemed suddenly small. A horrid thought began to dawn in her mind. As she gazed from one man to the other she knew the truth. Dare's eyes flicked her with disgust, then he nodded and walked from the room.

The musicians were still playing the slow, dreamy number and Don moved to pull Stephanie back into his arms. Stephanie was glad they were close to the door. She moved towards it, wanting to follow Dare, but Don's grip held her, forcing her back.

'Just an old friend of my . . .'

'Wife's?' finished Stephanie flatly.

She saw from his gesture her guess was correct.

'And do you have children?'

'Yes, three,' he admitted.

Stephanie saw the tall figure through the hall and knew Dare was leaving. She felt curiously numbed, as though someone else was living through the nightmare. The memory of that look of disgust which had shown her Dare's feelings seemed to have burnt itself like a brand. She waited for him to turn and look at her as he went out the door, but he glanced neither at her nor Don again. The door shut quietly behind him.

Don began speaking. 'Doll, we can work it out. Let's face it, we've both had such a good time tonight, don't let the fact of my marriage break it up. My wife knows I have to come here regularly on business, so she'll never find out. We can develop a really warm relationship, as the saying goes. I won't mention her, I promise. Out of sight is out of mind.'

The words penetrated into Stephanie's brain. She wondered why Don had seemed so charming earlier when he was so obviously without scruples.

'You make me sick,' she said quietly. 'I'm going home, Don. I want to be on my own. I advise you to go home to your wife.'

She moved away blindly, her feet taking her out the side door and into the garden. She noticed a back gate and realised that by following the narrow path she would end in the next street and soon she could be back at the flat. She didn't want to be seen with tears in her eyes.

Her footsteps sounded a quick tattoo as she walked towards her sanctuary. Once there she removed her gay golden sandals sadly. As always Dare's timing had been precise. He could hardly have seen her in a more damaging situation, she acknowledged. Obviously he thought she didn't care about the fact that Don was married.

A sharp peal on the doorbell startled her. Automatically she went to open it, then checked when she made out the outline of Don's sleek car outside. Slowly she put the door on the chain before she opened it the couple of inches the chain allowed.

'Doll, you don't understand—I'm crazy about you. Why did you leave the party? I've been looking for you.'

'Don, you know very well you allowed me to think you were single. Please go away, I don't want to see you again.'

Stephanie pictured the look of disgust on Dare's face and had no difficulty in shutting the door despite Don's pleadings.

'I'll stay out here till you do talk to me,' he threatened.

Stephanie knew that to open the door meant trouble. For the first time she regretted her decision to live alone. At least in the flat in Wellington such scenes would not have occurred. A hint of a smile crossed her face as she thought of her friend Mat, and her probable reaction. Guessing that Don would leave if he was ignored, she went off to have her shower and then climbed into bed. Her evening which she had looked forward to so much had turned into disaster.

Seeing Dare again and turned out even worse than in her nightmares. She wriggled deeper into the bed, wishing she could blot out the glance which had conveyed so much although so little had been said. It was unfortunate that she could imagine what Dare had thought; the subject gave her little peace. At last, after tossing and turning for another hour, she got up again and made herself a cup of hot chocolate. She took the drink into the lounge and was about to switch on the light when she stopped. Outside Don's car still stood.

Aghast, she looked around, but could see no sign of Don. He had evidently walked down the street to the nearby motels and left the car. It was just as well Dare did not know where she lived, she thought wryly. Don's car outside at three in the morning was damning evidence.

Knowing sleep was totally impossible, she picked up a book and started to read. When she woke in the morning it was late and she looked up bleary-eyed at the light, wondering why it was still switched on. Dare's image sprang to mind and with it the reminder of the events of the evening before. Hastily she fled from her bed to glance out the lounge window. Don's car was gone, and she relaxed. At least that was one problem solved, she told herself. She would not have to worry about Don turning up again.

Dare, of course, was a slightly different problem. In time she might be able to correct the impression he had gained the previous night, but added to their earlier quarrel it would be difficult. She decided to be cool and calm, and that way they could possibly meet without friction. For the sake of her family and his she had to make the attempt. After all, she reasoned, what she did was no longer of any concern to Dare Nayton.

'From now on I'll stick to a parrot and a cat!' she muttered. 'Though where you get a parrot from I'm not certain, and if I did, with my luck, it wouldn't last a day with the cat!'

Stephanie was glad to be back at work on Monday. The week settled into a routine, arranging and researching material, considering programmes, listening to tapes and editing others. She had her own studio times worked out well in advance and usually recorded her own interviews there, but sometimes it was necessary to take the recorder out to the subject. By the end of the week she had begun to put the incident at the party at the back of her mind. All the same, she didn't want to go home at the weekend. She didn't want to face Dare Nayton quite so soon.

The senior announcer walked into her office and Stephanie, seeing he carried the roster sheet, pointed him to a chair.

'Thanks, Stephanie. I've a bit of a problem on Saturday night. How do you feel about doing a straight air shift again? I know in the old days you weren't keen on Saturday night, but I wondered if you'd consider it?'

'For you? Of course!' Stephanie's eyes sparkled as she answered, thinking work would be a perfect excuse.

'It's the same as the old days, the formula you know.'

'Let's see—it's Beach and Barbecue until nine-thirty, then Party Scene until closedown at midnight,' recalled Stephanie.

'That's it!' said the announcer. 'How long is it since you've done a straight shift?'

'Not since I've left here,' she confessed. 'Over four years.'

'I'm on duty tonight. Come in when you've had tea and I'll go over the new equipment and you can have a rehearsal and a practice on the air with me.'

'That will be fine,' smiled Stephanie as the announcer wrote her name on to the roster.

'I'll put you down for the odd straight air shift in the next few weeks, if you like, Stephanie. We'll be a little short-handed as everybody wants to have holidays in summertime.' He pulled a lugubrious face.

'I'm only too happy to help out,' she said. 'Evening shifts in particular, but if I have to schedule an interview in a rostered time I'll come screaming. However, I should be able to avoid it.'

'That's fine, Stephanie. I'll see you tonight.'

That evening Stephanie slipped along to the station. It was oddly quiet walking along the empty corridor and even her own office looked deserted. She went straight to the studio area and there at least the lights and the music were normal. She pushed the heavy door and the announcer welcomed her.

'Got your headphones? Good. You can observe for a few minutes, then at eight o'clock we have a half-hour tape and you can have a try out while that's running. After that you do some on your own.'

Stephanie watched and listened. Once the eight o'clock programme was safely under way she experimented with the new tape machine. She operated it a few times until she felt reasonably confident. By the end of the shift at midnight she was announcing the discs with some of her old easy listening style, and the head was approving.

'That's great, Stephanie. I'll drop you off on my way home.'

Stephanie felt wide awake as she always did after an air shift. However, talking together outside the flat for a little while helped to calm her and by the time she switched off the light she felt almost sleepy. It was just as well there was no need for her to get up early in the morning, she thought thankfully. Later the next day she would be able to tidy the flat. Vaguely she remembered that moment the week before when the telephone call had shattered the peace she had held for so long. Since Dare's arrival her whole world seemed to have tilted dangerously.

'It's only old memories,' she told herself. 'He's not going to affect my life at all. At least,' she added, 'not if I have anything to say about it!'

CHAPTER TWO

THE total concentration forced on her by the demands of the work kept her thoughts away from Dare. Saturday's Party Scene work collected telephone requests, and that night there seemed more than usual. Her technician was extremely swift and she was glad as so much of the success of the programme depended on slick presentation. Although they hadn't done a shift together before, they soon adjusted to each other's style and by the end of the programme were able to know by a glance or an intonation just when to release the tapes or discs. In the earlier part they had been forced to use the cue lights, but Stephanie had disliked using them unless really necessary. It made her job so much easier to know the technician was interested and following the programme so intently. When she finally gave the closedown signal she pushed back the red microphone button with a feeling of satisfaction. She stretched widely, thrusting her arms back to ease the pressure on her back after sitting for so long. She had forgotten just how hard the announcer's chair could get despite its contoured cushions.

'Got your car, Stephanie?' queried the technician.

'No, I didn't bother, the flat is so close.'

'I'll give you a ride home as soon as I've finished here.'

'Thanks all the same, but I'd rather walk, honestly. It will help to settle me.'

'OK, Steph; that was a good programme.'

The compliment pleased her, coming from the technician.

'You did your part well!' she smiled, then gathered her papers together neatly and switched off the studio light. The thickly padded door closed silently after her and she let herself out into the main foyer. A minute later she began the walk home. She breathed deeply, then hummed quietly to herself. Her footsteps made a click-clack accompaniment to the last song and she tried to think of another tune which would fit in. At least, she reminded herself, this Saturday evening had passed less disastrously than the previous one, although she was walking home again at midnight.

Stephanie wasn't quite sure when she became aware that she was not the only pedestrian. As she crossed the street she saw two youths were following her and as she was due to turn into the darker side street which led to her flat she hesitated and looked around hopefully at the road. A car pulled up beside her. Glancing at the driver, she moved back, thinking she had thrown herself from the fat into the fire.

'Stephanie—hop in.'

'Dare, I'm almost home,' she explained, but looking at the two youths, who were now closer, decided her. She stepped into the car and had the satisfaction of seeing her pursuers left behind. Dare's glance at the driving mirror as he pulled the car on to the road told her he must have been aware of the potential situation.

'I'll go a slightly different way, it's too obvious just to go straight to the flat.'

'Thank you,' said Stephanie quietly. 'There was probably no danger.'

'No point in taking such risks, Stephanie.'

She studied him surreptitiously. His face was in the shadow, but his hands on the steering wheel were firm and looked capable. There was a small cut on the side of one hand, and she wondered how it had happened. She would have liked to have asked him how he just happened to be along at the right time. In the old days he would often turn up after the late shift and then they would sit and talk until she was sleepy. He would kiss her goodnight, with such tenderness, before he left to drive out to the farm, that they could hardly bear to part. Her lips twisted and she looked out the window fixedly, but she could not control the small tremor that ran through her.

'You're a bit shaken, Stephanie. I'll come in and see your flat's all right. Alan told me you live on your own.'

The car turned into the opposite end of her street and she noticed gratefully that there was no sign of the two youths.

'I'll be fine, Dare—I'm a big girl now, remember?'

Dare pulled the car up outside the flat and immediately walked round to open the door. Stephanie noticed the gesture. Dare's manners had always been polished. He escorted her to the door and calmly took the key from her suddenly nerveless fingers.

'Please come in,' Stephanie invited reluctantly, as she entered. 'I'll make a drink if you like.' She toyed nervously with the silver tea service on the buffet by the door.

'No, thanks.'

For a moment they looked at each other. Stephanie was conscious of her heartbeat speeding under the intensity of Dare's eyes.

'Patron of the right things brigade, Miss Stephanie

Fernley!' Dare mocked softly. 'It doesn't go with the other evidence. You look such an innocent, fragile flower too!'

Stephanie almost flinched from the bitter, hard note in his voice. She struggled for calm.

'Think what you like,' she said with an attempt to sound uncaring. She turned away and in an effort to seem relaxed she sat down on the floor and began unlacing her sandals.

'I generally do.'

Dare, to her consternation, seemed as if he was prepared to wait until she gave him her attention. Deliberately she straightened one slim leg and tucked it under her, then turned to the other sandal. She took her time, feeling Dare's gaze on her, and it took every ounce of willpower not to fumble the intricate laces. At last she looked up, and Dare continued,

'I was surprised about Don, though.'

'So was I.' Seeing Dare's look, she added hastily, 'I didn't know he was married.'

'So you decided to entertain him at home instead of at the party.'

Dare's voice lashed at her and Stephanie stood up, her intentions to remain calm forgotten.

'That's a rotten thing to say, Dare! His car may have been out front, but I assure you Don wasn't anywhere around.'

'It's a little late for the Miss Righteous act,' Dare said tightly. 'As you said, you're a big girl now.' He walked away, then deliberately retraced his footsteps. Stephanie let her head fall forward so he would not see the agony in her eyes. Dare must have realised, as he bent and turned her face round in his hands, his touch gentle.

'Sorry, Stephanie. I've been wanting to talk to you, but it can wait.'

'You might as well say what you like,' Stephanie began tiredly. The touch of Dare's hands on her face had awakened a host of thoughts that she wished could be forgotten.

'Not tonight,' said Dare quietly, then as though searching for a different topic he turned to the room. 'It looks quite a good flat, Stephanie.'

They might have been discussing the price of mushrooms or some other event of no appeal to them, she thought desperately.

'It's close to the studio,' she confirmed briefly.

Dare paced out the long blank wall thoughtfully and Stephanie watched, puzzled.

'I might have a picture for your wall,' he said at last.

Her surprise must have been obvious, as Dare's eyes gleamed.

'You haven't seen it. You might not be so pleased when you do. It was painted to lay a ghost.'

'And did it?' queried Stephanie, intrigued in spite of herself.

'No,' Dare admitted. 'But other events, places and people have.' He turned to go into the small hall. 'Perhaps we might be able to talk some other time. Goodnight, Stephanie.'

He let himself out and the door closed quietly after him.

It took Stephanie a long time to even move from her frozen position. Her thoughts about Dare's offer of the picture flared with hope like a bright firecracker, then died just as quickly.

As she went to her bedroom she wondered again how he

had just happened to be in the right street. What had he wanted to talk to her about? Could he have realised the possible explanations for their misunderstandings?

Her thoughts in turmoil, Stephanie sat on the edge of the bed. Gradually she calmed down. If Dare had indeed thought of some other answer to that dreadful mistake, he would have come straight out with it, demanding the truth. He wouldn't have waited four years.

She picked up the hairbrush and brushed her hair with unaccustomed severity. It was one way to forget the painful fact that the old chemistry was still strong. Dare's touch on her skin, the firmness of his lips, the easy graceful way he had of leaning lazily against the door-jamb, were achingly familiar. The bitter, hard anger was new, and recalling his icy look and his mocking 'Patron of the right things brigade', Stephanie felt torn. She couldn't understand him any longer, and the sooner she put him out of her mind the better.

Her glance fell on the little painting which Dare had done so long before. In it her eyes were wide and full of enchantment and mystery, staring back at her with a hint of humour. As she switched off the light, Stephanie wondered about the painting Dare had offered, recalling his reason for painting it. What had he meant? The thought teased her, but sheer exhaustion sent her to sleep.

By concentrating on work Stephanie managed to pass the following three weeks. She knew she was running away from seeing Dare, but she had been dismayed that the attraction was still so potent. After four years she had made her own life and she wasn't going to have the whole fabric shredded.

Weekends and evenings were made easier by working the occasional announcing shift, and they also served to give her an excuse for not going home. She enjoyed herself entertaining several of her friends to dinner and went to the movies and the theatre too. Reasonably certain she could remain calm and unmoved the next time she met Dare, she was shocked to discover that the opposite happened.

With a group of friends she went to the Court Theatre to see one of Shakespeare's plays. She studied the programme, checking the list of familiar favourites, as they waited for the prologue. An expectant hush as the theatre darkened made her look up. Seated across the aisle was a tall, dark-haired figure. He turned and their eyes met. The storm scene that followed seemed to Stephanie to be singularly appropriate. As the black-robed figures fulfilled their tragic destiny Stephanie risked another glance at Dare. He seemed to be engrossed in the action, though the blonde girl beside him seemed more interested in him. Swiftly, Stephanie glued her eyes back on the stage, conscious that her raging emotions were mirrored there. She pressed her hands into each other to still their trembling. The moment the play had finished she made a hasty retreat. As she started her car the sight of Dare escorting his girl-friend across the road made her moment of relief shortlived. It was good to reach the privacy of her flat, but once there the thought mocked her.

'This weekend I'm going home,' she told herself. 'I'm tired. That's all it is, just fatigue. It's just a hangover from the days when we used to love each other. If I ignore it the problem will disappear.'

In the morning Stephanie spoke to her mother and told

her she would be home that evening after finishing work. Ironically her mother mentioned that Dare was to be away on a painting trip. Magically Stephanie found herself singing at the full power of her lungs as she drove home. After receiving a very odd look from an approaching car she decided that perhaps her voice was louder than she realised. The thought caused her lips to curve and her eyes to sparkle. When she drove through the farm gates a few minutes later her mother and father were there to meet her.

'Darling, it's good to have you home again!'

'Thought you'd forgotten about us,' teased her father. 'Must be some boy-friend you've got in town.'

'No, just work, Dad,' she managed a wry grin. 'It's good to be home.'

She breathed deeply of the fresh clean air. The bleat of the sheep and the soft, low enquiry from a cow by the fence seemed wonderfully familiar.

'I seem to have been away for ages,' she agreed. 'Mum, your garden is looking beautiful.'

The whole weekend was idyllic. She did very little, content to sit in the sun and swim in the pool.

'We'll have to close the pool soon,' remarked Alan thoughtfully. 'It's been a long season this year.'

'Not just yet—after all, it's still enjoyable.'

'You're as bad as Dare! He's down here most evenings when he isn't in town with his girl-friend.'

The casually spoken words struck sharply at Stephanie, and she turned in surprise. 'Dare has a girl-friend?'

'Dare's always had girl-friends, but this one is special. Smashing-looking, of course, a blonde as a matter of fact. She only got back from overseas a few weeks back. Came from Nelson, but her parents moved South about six months ago. Dare met her in Greece. We went out in a foursome last week.'

Stephanie floated in the pool, struggling not to show the feelings which raced through her. Alan, oblivious of the effect of his words, hauled himself out of the pool. She dared not ask her brother for further details but told herself that it was only natural that Dare should have a special girl. She remembered the blonde she had seen with Dare earlier. Immediately she began wondering how she would cope when she met the 'smashing' girl, then told herself that as she had successfully stayed away from Dare over the past few weeks there would be little difficulty.

Dare had made no effort to contact her or to drop the promised painting into the flat, and she guessed that he had decided to avoid her, or that he had forgotten. Either was unusual, but easily explained now that his girl-friend had returned.

There was no singing as Stephanie drove soberly back to town on Monday morning. She was glad work was as fast paced as always with news interviews and local personalities. On Wednesday she was late after finishing an interview at six o'clock and she went straight to the flat. Once she had put away the recorder she undid her sandals. The simple task reminded her of Dare watching her unlace the long leather thongs. The peal of the door bell startled her, and she answered it automatically, one sandal in her hand.

'Don!' she exclaimed.

'Stephanie, please.'

Don walked in despite her shocked expression. Slowly she followed him into the room.

'Darling, you look as though you were posing for Cinderella,' he drawled.

'Well, as far as I'm concerned, you're not the handsome prince,' Stephanie said.

'Stephanie, grow up, doll! What my wife doesn't know can't hurt her. I'm here for two nights. Let's live it up.'

'Stop, Don! Don't make it worse. There are names I could call you, but it would be insulting to members of the insect world.'

'All right, all right!' His handsome face looked petulant. 'I'm going. I thought you might have seen a little sense if I left you for a while.'

He moved to the door and she held it open for him. To her chagrin he bent and took a kiss from her outraged lips.

'I still think you're the most entrancing-looking doll. I'll be back in four weeks and staying at the same motel, so you can leave a message.' He straightened his jacket and moved off to his car.

Stephanie seethed with anger as he left. Only then did she notice another car pulled up behind Don's. Even as the tall, lean figure approached she knew instinctively that he had witnessed Don's leavetaking, and the anger that she had felt seconds before turned to despair. She stood dumbly as Dare, carrying a large painting, entered the flat.

His face was taut and hard and his eyes were like chips from the blue glaciers. None too gently he put the painting down.

'This was waiting for you at the farm. I thought I would have seen you before.'

His words were clipped and Stephanie knew he was furious but trying not to show it.

'Thank you for bringing it in. I've been working all the weekends up till last weekend. It's kind of you to give it to me.' She knew she was sounding oddly formal and she instinctively put out a hand to touch his in a pleading gesture.

'Dare, that's the first time I've seen Don since that night you returned. He was only here for one minute.'

'You're not answerable to me, Stephanie,' interrupted Dare, with a touch of cool hauteur.

He turned on his heel and walked out, leaving the large painting propped by the wall. With the hint of tears in her eyes Stephanie moved from the door. Only blind fate could have led to the two men calling so inopportunely.

The painting was wrapped, and she wondered as she slowly sat down and untied the other sandal what it would reveal. A gay voice interrupted her melancholy mood.

'Stephanie, cooee!'

'Mat! Come in, I need some company. I'll put the kettle on.' With a quick gesture Stephanie thrust her troubles behind her. 'Here's a seat Mat—have you walked all the way?'

'Yes, I'm meant to take so much exercise walking and as it was such a pleasant evening I thought I'd come this far. Ray's probably wondering where I've got to,' Mat laughed.

'Give him a ring while I make the tea. Tell Ray to come as well and we can have a meal together.'

'Sounds a lovely idea. I'll tell Ray to bring some food.'

'Nonsense, I've plenty here as I went out to the farm and I've brought back a supply. I made a casserole last night ready for today as I knew I'd be working late and there's so much of it I thought I'd have to deep-freeze it. And I haven't really the room in my freezer!'

Stephanie switched on the oven and prepared a few more potatoes. As they were cooking the two girls had their tea. As she put down the silver tea service she had used, Stephanie's mouth drooped as she remembered Dare's comment, 'Patron of the right things brigade'.

'What's up, Stephanie?' asked Mat. 'It's not like you to be down in the dumps.'

'You're too observant, Mat.'

'It's just that I'm very fond of you and you've been working as though time's run away lately. Was it anything to do with the dark-haired man I saw leaving?'

Stephanie nodded. 'That was Dare Nayton.'

'Dare? Where have I heard that name before? I remember.' Mat paused suddenly. 'Wasn't he the special man in your life when you first came to Wellington?' Her question was gentle.

'Something like that,' Stephanie agreed. 'We had a break and he went overseas, now he's returned. It's just opened an old wound, I suppose. I thought I'd forgotten.'

'Tell me about it. At the time you never said a word. But I hardly knew you then.'

'That's right, I'd only just moved into the flat. Although Dare and I were not officially engaged, we were both saving to get married. It seems stupid now, but when I first went to Wellington I wanted Dare to write to me before I wrote to him. I didn't get a letter and I began wondering if he really was in love after all. And then I started working with Goldie on evening work interviews and spending a lot of time with him. We really were working, but it was just unfortunate that Dare rang about four times in a row and I was always out with Goldie. In my letters home I mentioned that he was a bachelor and a real city slicker, and of course Alan passed on the letter to Dare. I'd also mentioned someone called Mat in the letter Dare read and said I was thinking about moving in with this character who was a football fanatic.'

'Oh, no!'

Stephanie looked at her friend with a grimace. 'I told you it was silly! Dare read it and got the wrong idea. In my next letter I told them I'd moved in with Mat, who also worked in broadcasting, and we were sharing a flat with the most glorious views in Wellington, and I was spending all Saturdays watching footie and Mat was fantastic. I did say that I missed the family.' Stephanie pulled a face and added, 'I didn't want to write that I missed Dare—my stupid pride wouldn't allow that. At any rate the family were pretty upset, imagining that I'd been carried off by some great rugby forward. Dad pointed out that mixed flatting didn't necessarily imply a sexual relationship, so they all calmed down. My next letter raved on about the view from our bedroom, and that rather made nonsense of Dad's idea.

'When Dare read it he decided to fly up immediately to Wellington. He was furiously angry and probably very hurt. Unfortunately, he arrived the morning after that twenty-first party of yours.' She stopped for a moment, reflecting.

'Oh, Stephanie, talk about a comedy of errors! I shouldn't be smiling, I really am the most unsympathetic of friends.' Mat's eyes twinkled. 'I think I can guess the rest. I was on early shift that morning and a group of us had gone straight to work from the party, leaving you behind. Surrounded by bottles and glasses and debris from supper! I suppose he thought you were completely bohemian.'

'Plus the fact that after I waved you lot off, I decided to climb into my oldest gear and begin tidying. I'd actually cleared the lounge by the time Dare arrived. You can imagine how I felt by ten o'clock after being up all night. I was tired, my mascara had run all over the place, my hair looked a mess tied back in a scarf like some caricature of Mrs Mopp.'

'I can just picture it!'

'I hadn't started on the bedroom as your young brother was fast asleep in there. He'd brought a sleeping bag, but as neither you nor I had used the beds he decided to make himself more comfortable. While I was cleaning he was snoring away.'

'Sounds like my young brother,' put in Mat. 'He believes in making himself at home.'

'Then the doorbell went. I thought one of the techs had come back to give me a hand with cleaning up, so I shouted out to come in. So Dare did. I don't know what he thought, but we couldn't move when we saw each other. I was so surprised to see him and I think he probably thought I looked terrible. I didn't know what to do, he looked so angry. I panicked. I showed him into the lounge and pointed out the view, then dragged him off to see the view from the bedroom—remember, it was much better than from the lounge, as the tree didn't block it. I'd forgotten about your brother.

'He woke up just as Dare and I walked in. His shirt and pants were flung over the wardrobe door and of course he wasn't wearing a pyjama top. The dressing table had the word "Terrific" written in lipstick across the mirror.'

'I remember, one of the young techs had written it when they all trooped in to look at the view. I nearly killed him for using my lipstick!' said Mat.

'Dare took one look and said, "I presume this is Mat". Your brother smiled and said, "No, I'm the baby brother. It's all right, it's all in the family".'

Stephanie paused. 'He meant it to be a reassuring remark, but it wasn't the way the evidence looked and sounded. Dare didn't say a word. He just looked at me and walked out. He returned to the farm, packed his bags and went overseas.'

'Oh, Stephanie, why didn't you tell me?' exclaimed Mat. 'I could have explained. It was all so innocent.'

Seeing her friend's stricken face Stephanie managed a smile. 'It was my own fault. I should have written to Dare in the first place. I thought I'd explained that your name was short for Matilda when I wrote home. You see, I wasn't able to understand why Dare had reacted so badly. I was furious with him for jumping to conclusions about your young brother, so I wouldn't tell him just how wrong he was. It wasn't till I went home and Mum asked me about you that I got some glimmer of understanding. I saw her face when I told her you were going out with Ray and that's when I knew what had happened. By then Dare had been overseas six months.'

'And what does Dare think of the whole mix-up now? I guess you've had a few laughs over it?'

Stephanie shook her head. 'He doesn't know. I had hoped to be able to tell him, but I left it too late. Now, of course, he thinks I'm having an affair with Don.'

'The guy from Timaru?'

'That's right. Dare saw his car outside my flat on the night of the party and just now he saw Don kiss me as he left the flat. What he didn't see was Don arrive about two minutes before, and I certainly didn't kiss him. You see, Don's married.'

'What a muddle! I think you'd better stick to Goldie,' smiled Mat. 'On the other hand, perhaps Dare wants to make it up. He's given you this painting, so perhaps this is your chance.'

'No, he told me he painted it to lay a ghost and I wouldn't care for it.'

Almost as if her movements were being shown in slow motion Stephanie moved towards the picture and carefully took off the protective cover. From a distance she heard Mat gasp as the vividness of the painting filled the room.

Instinctively Stephanie stood back, and then realised the painting was in three sections, broken by three window frames. The first was an almost idyllic replica of the pastel in her bedroom except that the face of the child was a blank mask. The second was a swirling series of vivid blocks and traces of silver threads which could have been a woman's body but might not have been. The third was a scene that both girls recognised together.

'Our bedroom!'

'Surely it never looked so . . .'

'Tacky?' supplied Stephanie bitterly. 'It probably did the morning after that party.'

'There's even something written on the mirror.'

'Terrific,' Stephanie supplied.

Her friend misunderstood. 'You're right! It's a fascinating painting. Oh, Stephanie, he must have been madly in love with you to have painted this picture. You used to have a watercolour like this first one, didn't you? I can remember it.'

'It's in my bedroom,' Stephanie commented, her eyes still drawn to the centre panel.

'I'll get Ray to help you to hang it. I'm afraid it's a bit out of my reach at the moment.'

'I'm not sure I even want to put it up,' said Stephanie.

'You couldn't bear not to, I imagine there are all sorts of details which you'll only pick up after you've studied it quite a lot. Look at the line of those chestnut trees in the background of the picture with you.'

The sound of a cheerful call interrupted them, and a moment later Ray was studying the picture too.

'Don't know the first thing about painting, Stephanie, but this is impressive,' he admitted. 'Where's a hammer and some picture hooks? It'll go well in that space.'

A few moments later he stepped down, and all three of them stared at the picture.

'That centre one looks like a nightclub.'

'You're right, Ray, possibly all that frenetic movement is a dancer,' put in Mat.

'Or a mistake with a pot of paint,' said Stephanie, with an attempt at a joke. 'I'll get dinner.'

Later, after Ray and Mat had left, Stephanie stared at the centre panel again. The sun had almost dropped out of sight and a lonely beam lit the pattern, shifting the accents and colours. Immediately Stephanie saw with a stark reality that Dare had painted the scene from the Wellington flat window, the blue of the harbour, the silver threads of the curving rail lines, the grey of the streets and the blocks of the skyscrapers. They were plainly revealed on the dancer's skirt, and she wondered how she had not seen it before. Just as suddenly the sunbeam vanished and the panel changed again. It was, Stephanie decided, as elusive as the painter, the enigmatic Dare Nayton.

CHAPTER THREE

STEPHANIE had barely arrived at work the next morning when her telephone blipped softly.

'Good morning, Stephanie Fernley speaking.'

'Stephanie, I'm calling from Wellington. I'm flying down tomorrow to go over some special material for a series I'm thinking about—on travellers, possible title "Footloose but not Free".'

'Sounds interesting, Goldie. It's good to hear you. What time will you be here?'

'I'll be arriving at the station about one o'clock.'

'I'll look forward to it.'

As she put down the receiver Stephanie smiled. Goldie was always pleasant and his observations worth listening to at any time. She flicked through her files to see if she could remember any recent travellers and made several notes. Almost unbidden came the thought of Dare Nayton. For such a programme he would be perfect. She grimaced at the thought of interviewing the owner of those cold blue eyes. She would sooner do an interview in a lion's cage than interview Dare!

Putting on a tape to edit, she made a few notes; the speaker, a local man with a passion for archaeology, had spent most of his holidays digging up past Maori *pa* sites. In his own way he was an individualist, and his comments had wit. Although probably not what Goldie had intended, he would be suitable for the proposed programme. When she had finished editing it to the length she needed for her session, she collated a number of research notes about her next subject, a North American trade expert. The interview turned out to be more difficult than she had imagined as the expert was convincing on a number of points of interest to the Canterbury farmer. It was like having four fish to catch and only one rod and one hook, she thought ruefully. She realised the subject's comments could have a place in the rural programme section, and the extra hook provided her with time. Stephanie was glad her farming background had provided her with the slant.

She was listening to the replay the next day when Goldie arrived. He was a person who was easy to relax with, and she would always be grateful for his helpful advice when she had first begun training.

'Come out to dinner with me, tonight?' he invited.

'I'll do better. I cooked a casserole after you phoned yesterday, so it shouldn't take long to heat through.'

'Stephanie, that's a wonderful idea. We can go on working over dinner.'

Goldie's enthusiasm matched her own, she conceded, when he finally took his leave. The dinner had been briefly praised, Goldie speculating on the merits of a programme about methods of cookery almost in passing. The only time when they hadn't talked shop had been when Goldie had walked into the flat and been spellbound by the painting. It was only with difficulty that she had avoided his questions about the artist, and she noticed that several times his eyes drifted back to the painting, then to her, as though comparing each line.

Although Stephanie was early at work the next morning, Goldie was ahead of her, and he greeted her with a quietness which made her study him.

'Stephanie, that painting's been at the back of my mind all night. The artist is good. Tell me, why did he sign it Anon? Who is he?'

'His initials are ANON—Adair Neil Oliver Nayton,' Stephanie explained. 'It was a joke when we were children. He used to call me "little bug" or "Staphylococcus". He was just the boy next door.'

'Would that be Dare Nayton? He created quite a sensation overseas with some of his work last year. I didn't realise he was back. You should interview him, Stephanie.'

'I'd rather not,' she said flatly.

'Why? Is he still in love with you?'

'No, of course not.' Stephanie was shocked by Goldie's perception.

'But you are still in love with him?'

'That's ridiculous—I've hardly seen Dare Nayton for four years!' She looked away from Goldie's kindly eyes.

'You know where to find me if you need me, Stephanie. We make a good team, you and I. Now let's get on with the tapes,' he continued.

Goldie liked quite a few of the ideas she had for the programme. After he had left she sat at her desk trying to sort out her feelings. Goldie was sweet, as she told Mat, but her attitude stopped there. She felt none of the shaking tremors which reduced her to pulp the moment Dare touched her.

The weekend seemed long in coming. She wanted to go home; partly, she had to admit, because she wanted to see Dare and perhaps have the chance to talk things out, and partly because she knew that if she stayed away another weekend Dare's parents and her own might think it strange.

Driving home in the heat of the Friday evening, she thought longingly of the swimming pool. At least there she could feel refreshed and perhaps the lethargy she had felt would dissipate. Only then did she remember her mother telling her that Alan and her parents were going to a clearing sale on Friday and would be late home.

The thought of the solitude did not worry her and she was feeling lighthearted as she changed in her bedroom into a scanty bikini and ran out to the pool. The water touched icy on her skin and she lowered herself gently into the water, savouring the almost sensual satin of the pool.

'You do that most elegantly.'

The voice speaking from the semi-dark startled her and she took a sudden mouthful of water, choking and spluttering.

Still coughing, she faced the bronzed figure. 'Dare Nayton, you scared me to death!'

'Don't exaggerate!' His voice had lost its usual coldness. 'Think what a visual temptation you offered me. It was a very pretty display, not one I needed, mind you. I'm quite well aware of your attractions.'

'Dare, you're insufferable!'

Dare's rich laughter cut short her indignant phrase.

'Now I know you're all right. Come on, I'll race you to the other end.'

Stephanie launched herself and swam strongly, but Dare caught her easily. He grinned at her with a boyish triumph as she conceded.

'I'll give you a head start.'

This time Stephanie stretched herself to the limit and she felt her body speed through the water. She touched the other end and stood to glance round, sure that she had won, but Dare was smiling lazily down at her.

'I had a lot of practice in Greece.'

She flung a handful of water at him and he retaliated. To avoid it Stephanie dived and surfaced some distance away. Dare dived after her, but she watched his shadow under the water, then leapt over him to reach the other side. Dare turned and caught her and she ended up in his arms. The touch of their wet bodies was like a physical shock and they both stared at each other with a hungry intensity. With a sudden shiver Stephanie turned and swam to the other end, and for a few moments there was only the steady splash of their arms as they moved in a tight race like lines up and down the pool. After she had completed several lengths she hauled herself out and wrapped her towel around her.

She was aware of Dare in the water, his attitude apparently relaxed. He reminded her of a tiger she had seen once. It had laid back somnolently and only the gaze of its eyes gave away its readiness to act. She had a sudden vision of Dare moving just as swiftly. In a sudden flurry she almost scuttled inside to change and found her breathing sounded loud in her ears. By the time she had finished her shower and taken her time over dressing she was sure Dare would have disappeared.

Obviously he had not been expecting her and for a few minutes they had been able to enjoy each other's company without antagonism. Delaying for a while longer, she peeped out at the pool, but its surface was unrippled by any motion. Half relieved, yet disappointed, she marched

out to the kitchen. Dare stood there, leaning against th
door-jamb, in the familiar stance.

'Thought it would be breakfast before you were coming
Hurry up and I'll give you some dinner at my place.'

Stephanie looked back at him, torn between the desir
to accept and yet certain that if she went she would end u
only more heartsore. Would this be the time to straighte
out their misunderstandings?

'Don't look so doubtful, the cooking's not that bad,' h
teased.

Remembering that Dare's mother was a splendid cook
she hastily apologised, 'Sorry, I didn't mean that.'

'Look, Stephanie, let's call a truce,' said Dare. 'W
won't discuss the past tonight. Some day, but not now.'

Stephanie nodded. Dare held out his hand and she pu
hers into it. The intimacy of the gesture reassured her. I
was a gesture of trust. In just such a protective way Dar
had taken her by the hand on the way to school for the firs
time. It was almost like a slap when he dropped it agair
almost immediately.

The gathering dark lay over the paddocks. Dare strode
out, whistling cheerfully and evidently totally at ease
Stephanie wished she could appear just as nonchalant. A
least at dinner Dare's parents would make the mooc
easier. She could see the twinkle of the farmhouse lights
through the trees ahead, and hoped it was a good omen
Perhaps she was wrong to risk this time with Dare, she
thought. Perhaps after all they could be calm and rationa
about the years they had been separated. But her hear
sounded a warning.

'We go this way,' Dare indicated the path to the old
barn.

'But the house is this way.'

'My house isn't,' answered Dare cryptically.

There wasn't room to walk two abreast and she was forced to follow along the path. Ahead of them the old barn stood, and even in the fast fading light Stephanie could see changes. She stopped and stared. The two-storey old brick shed had been almost entirely altered. One whole wall was now glass and the old balcony had been extended and strengthened.

'My studio's on the ground floor and the living area above,' Dare explained.

'That's incredible,' breathed Stephanie. 'It looks like something out of one of those trendy architect's magazines.'

'There's still quite a lot to be done, like the terrace outside and a spa pool, but I've moved in.'

He slid back an aluminium and glass door.

'Come in.'

Stephanie remembered the nursery rhyme about the spider and the fly and hesitated.

'Just a moment and I'll put the light on.'

In wonder she gazed around her. She could recognise the old shed easily now as the lights showed a large, virtually empty floor space. Along the back of one brick wall, racks and cupboards had been fitted. Two easels stood at angles to each other. On the floor an elaborate sheepskin rug was the only softening influence at the other end of the room. At the corner a staircase led to the upper floor.

'The glass means I can take advantage of the Canterbury light. Until I went overseas I never realised the strength of the sky here, the openness of the plains, and the

sculptured fullness of the hills.' Dare spoke softly, reflectively. 'I wondered what was wrong until I went to the
villages and knew I was missing the countryside.'

'Just a country boy,' mimicked Stephanie in a slow
Western drawl.

Dare's laughter echoed from the dark-stained rafters.

'You put in stairs,' pointed Stephanie. 'And two larger
windows at the back.'

'Right. That was one of the tricky bits. I wanted the
light. Fortunately the builder and I managed to work it
satisfactorily. The structure itself was sound as a bell and
needed very little imagination to see its potential.'

He climbed the stairs and, still large-eyed, Stephanie
followed. A short hall opened out and Dare flicked open a
door.

'Study, office, what you will.' It was a neat little room
with a desk, a comfortable chair and a divan. 'Opposite is
my bedroom and bathroom, I'm pleased with how they
worked out.'

Stephanie peeped in. The brick wall and the pale wood
of the joinery formed an attractive combination. A large
bed with a simple matching wood frame and a deep green
cover woven with russet formed the main feature. One
entire partition was bare and she glanced away from the
bed, hurriedly commenting on the unfinished area.

'What about a wall hanging on plaster?' she asked.

'Possibly, I decided on that in the lounge. If I can't find
something I might fill it up myself. Trouble is, I'd lie in
bed and keep seeing improvements! Then I'd have to hop
out and keep adding to it.' He grinned, a trace of the boy
she had known for so long, laughing at himself.

'Bathroom,' he announced.

Stephanie gasped.

'There's no roof, I can see the stars!'

'Not quite, merely glass over this section. I know I've got the spa going in downstairs, but I decided I might as well have the effect up here too.'

'It's incredible—positively sybaritic!'

Her fingers smoothed the luxurious towels, as her eyes took in the glittering fittings. She had seen pictures of fabulous bathrooms, but this one would have given pleasure to a Caesar.

'Kitchen and living out this way,' Dare commented, and rather weakly Stephanie followed as he led the way.

The kitchen area was compact and yet seemed to contain every device under its gleaming cupboards. Glass from head to waist level along the four sides gave a view into the lounge or out to the fields.

Dare took out a dish from the refrigerator and a pan from the cupboard. Even as she watched he proceeded to cook a Chinese style meal and the vapours were whisked away by the hood over the cooking area.

'Have a look round in the lounge—not much furniture yet.'

Stephanie smiled when she looked into the room and saw that again the floor surface was empty except for the one large sheepskin similar to the one on the studio floor. The brick walls were bare, apart from a dramatic wall hanging in wool, in natural colours representing in semi-abstract the land and sky. She spent some time studying it wordlessly, recognising the artistry involved.

'I bought it at a gallery a long time ago,' Dare told her, and handed her a drink, before he returned to the kitchen.

'It took me a while to decide where I wanted it; here, my bedroom or the studio.'

'It's magnificent,' acknowledged Stephanie. 'The whole place is unbelievable.'

She walked to the glass door which opened on to the balcony and sat for a while at the outdoor table and chairs Dare had there. She guessed that he would breakfast there, looking out to the mountains of the Southern Alps, in the distance. She moved back inside and shut the sliding door gently; it was cold outside with a hint of the Antarctic in the wind. The wind had changed completely from the earlier pleasantly hot breath of the north.

'Too cold to eat out there?' Dare queried.

''Fraid so.'

'Sorry, you'll have to manage on your lap on the mat.'

Stephanie sank down into the richness of the soft sheepskin. It seemed strange to think Dare could have recognised so much potential in the old shed they had spent so many hours in as youngsters. She recalled sliding down the hay bales, getting thistles in her bottom for her pains and doing gymnastics on the floor once the hay had gone.

It was incredible that it could be the same yet so different. She watched Dare move around in the kitchen and the past four years seemed to have disappeared. When he served her with a steaming platter of food she ate hungrily, appreciating the taste.

'Mmm, very good,' she smiled.

'Pour the coffee, will you, Stephanie, I'll just fix this up.'

It was hard to remain cool in the small space of the kitchen. They had barely talked during the meal, but Stephanie had been aware of Dare's long legs beside her.

She found the coffee mugs and admired their shape. Seeing her interest, Dare spoke.

'A friend of mine, Barbara Wade, who's a potter, made them for me. She's done a good job, don't you think?'

Stephanie swallowed hard, knowing instinctively that Dare was referring to the girl Alan had described as a 'real smasher'.

'Beautiful,' she agreed, struggling against the feelings which ripped through her.

'She hasn't been back from overseas long, either. I met her in Greece, of all places.'

'Romantic?'

'I suppose it was—blue skies, blue sea and a beautiful girl. We seemed to be always running into each other after that.'

Stephanie tried to find a smile.

'How nice,' she said politely.

'Wasn't it?' agreed Dare.

She flashed a glance at him and the impish look on his face reminded her of a thousand other teasing times.

'But we weren't going to talk of the past, were we?' he said smoothly, with the blandness of cream.

'That only leaves the future.'

'Not entirely—you forget the present,' said Dare as he lowered himself on to the rug beside her. He reached back and some music hummed from speakers she only now noticed, set high in each corner.

'I'll have to get some cushions,' put in Dare thoughtfully. 'Gold and amber and chestnut.'

Stephanie wasn't sure whether the remark was meant as a comment or a compliment. She wrapped the gold of her skirt around her legs, feeling oddly vulnerable. It was ridiculous she reasoned, to feel so tense, so conscious of Dare's masculinity. Deliberately she stretched out and casually leaned an elbow on the rug, her hand propping her head. At least it would make Dare think he did not affect her in any way, she told herself.

'So you're going to stay, Dare. Your parents will be pleased.'

'Yes, I can give Dad a hand and still have time for my work.'

'I know Mum, Dad and Alan are thrilled you're home.'

'But not you, Stephanie,' Dare said quietly.

'I didn't say that.'

'But it's the truth.'

Stephanie looked up at Dare and noticed his eyes were suddenly cold.

'Yes,' she admitted.

'I didn't think it would matter to you any longer. It seems out of character,' he added softly.

Tension seemed to make the air electric between them. Stephanie found herself at a complete disadvantage and she sat up abruptly. Her movement broke the spell.

'But you don't know me very well, Dare.'

'Well enough!' he answered shortly.

Suddenly she felt desperately tired, as though she had just finished a double shift. She looked up and found Dare's eyes on her. The old attraction was double-edged, she thought with a pang, like despair. She knew she could take no more.

'I'm going home,' she announced. The few hours they had spent so easily seemed to have already become a thing of the past. She stood up and Dare politely assisted her.

'I'll see you get back safely.'

'Don't bother,' Stephanie said quietly. 'I know the way.'

She brushed past him, almost running in her desire to leave the atmosphere which had built up so swiftly. Her feet flew down the stairs to the darkened studio and she had to pause to find the door. She took a moment for her eyes to adjust to the light and Dare approached as her fingers found the handle.

'It slides,' he commented, and stretched an arm around her to open the door.

Dare's jacket was slung over his arm and the coolness of the leather brushed her skin. She felt herself trapped by the door and the nearness of his body, and in almost a panic she turned to face him.

His eyes wore an unreadable expression and Stephanie caught her breath as he prevented her from moving away by tightening his arms around her. His lips were cynically twisted and she instinctively moved her head away as he bent to kiss her. His hand clamped firmly around her head, forcing her lips to meet the full onslaught of his mouth in a hard, bruising kiss. There was so much anger and passion that the kiss seemed to last for ever. Stephanie felt herself held more gently, before Dare's lips claimed hers again, but this time it was a more tender touch. Her arms slipped around him and she dared to hope that somehow a miracle had happened. Her whole being soared as the kiss deepened and their feelings exploded. A thousand stars shot through her and she heard herself whispering his name as she caressed the tiny spot at the back of his neck.

When he did not respond she opened her eyes. She almost reeled as at the same time he pushed her away.

'Terrific!' he said slowly, as though analysing her performance.

It took a moment for the meaning of the word to sink in, she was still too overwhelmed by the cataclysmic effect he had wrought on her. She felt herself stagger against the sharp edge of the door. The cool night air rushed against her. Her breathing came raggedly as she stumbled down the steps and broke into a run along the path. She was too shocked to question or demand explanations; all she could think about was the shock of the hurtful, ugly, deliberate insult. Vaguely she knew Dare was following her, but he made no attempt to catch her up.

As Stephanie let herself into her home she was glad the rest of the family were still out. It was unusual for them to be away so late, but she guessed they had stopped to see friends. Gratefully she closed her door and climbed into bed. Even there the sorrow and anguish was almost too much. Her chest felt as if someone had placed an enormous iron weight upon it, and her gasps of pain only gradually turned into sobs. Sheer emotional exhaustion caused her to feel numbed before she finally slept.

The clink of dishes and the aroma of cooking woke her. Almost at once the memory of the night before flashed before her eyes. Lying in bed, she could fragment the scenes, seeing Dare as the playful swimmer, then the charming host delighting in his new home and the companionable raconteur. She shook her head as she recalled the way he had forced that first kiss, then expertly fanned her feelings, and the coolly dispassionate way he had contemptuously dismissed her. The finality of that 'Terrific', burnt.

Stephanie heard her mother's footsteps in the hall and a moment later her door opened.

'Good morning, darling, did you sleep well? You look a little drawn. All this work lately! Stay in bed this morning and rest. We had a lovely time yesterday. Your father is pleased, he managed to get the items he was after at a fair price and I picked up a few oddments too. I never can resist auctions—it's such a challenge!'

Stephanie smiled. Her mother's ability to chatter on had undergone a fair chaffing in the family, but Stephanie found it a balm on this occasion.

'I saw a screen too that I nearly bought for Dare. It was such a lovely big one.' She stopped and put her hand to her mouth. 'Oh, my goodness, I've spoiled the surprise! Oh, Stephanie, I know Dare wanted to tell you himself.' Mrs Fernley looked contrite.

'About the house? I saw it last night, Mum.'

'Oh, good! I had a bet with Alan that I could refrain from comment about it until you saw it for yourself.' Her mother smiled again. 'Tell me what you thought of the studio?'

'It's superb,' Stephanie admitted truthfully. 'I couldn't believe it.'

'We couldn't believe it when Dare told us his plans for it. I thought perhaps he'd let his imagination run riot. Even your father had his doubts, and it wasn't till he saw the blueprints that he understood. And of course, Dare was lucky with the builders.'

'It must have been done in record time,' commented Stephanie.

'Yes, they happened to have had a delay in a project they were due to start on and Dare could offer them a tempting sum. I believe he must have done better than we realised overseas. Of course, Dare was never one to blow his own trumpet,' Mrs Fernley added reflectively. 'Darling, you're not eating the breakfast I brought you!' she added.

'Sorry, Mum, I just couldn't face food this morning—perhaps I over-ate last night.'

Stephanie didn't feel like telling her mother that discussion of the wonderful abilities of their neighbour had turned the toast to cold ash in her mouth.

'Which reminds me, you didn't have any of the food I left ready for you.'

'Dare provided it,' Stephanie explained.

'That would have been pleasant for the two of you. Dare has some fascinating tales. I'm never quite sure sometimes if he's pulling my leg or not. Some of his stories are so outrageous. Fun, though. Did he tell you about the girl in London and the cat? I still chortle whenever I think about it.'

Stephanie managed to wriggle around and her mother took the hint. 'That's right, dear, you cuddle down and have a sleep.'

Stephanie felt a fraud hiding herself under the blankets, but her nerve ends were jumping each time her mother mentioned Dare's name. The thought of Dare and another girl, with or without a cat, awoke a storm of feelings. She knew it was ridiculous. Dare had probably had many girl-friends and she, Stephanie Fernley, was not going to waste another thought on the man.

She jumped out of bed in resolution. She knew she could not stay there letting her thoughts stray. She would not suddenly depart for her flat, as that would hurt her mother, but at least she could keep busy and in doing so stop thinking about Dare—and the shattering experiences of the night before.

She dressed in an old pair of shorts, sun-top and a large straw hat and set out for the garden. The long bed by the fence was overdue for attention, she decided with pleasure. As she forked and weeded and clipped she ruthlessly pushed away the invading memories. By lunchtime she had worked up an appetite and in her family's company there was a need to sound normal. To her relief they were discussing the advantages of a new truck, so she had little need to pass comment. Afterwards she returned to the garden. She viewed her efforts with pleasure until she realised that a couple of the trees had a branch in the wrong place. The loppers were in the garden shed and they were razor-sharp.

'There, Dare Nayton!' announced Stephanie as she put power into a particularly obtruding branch. It fell with a satisfying whish and she proceeded to the next one almost with glee.

'Off with his head,' she said as another branch flopped earthwards. 'Down with all artists, and one in particular!' she announced, as she raised the loppers again and sighted another which could do with a trim. It was easy to clear a few more, she decided, as well as being satisfying therapy.

Her arms were aching when she finally returned the loppers to their place, but the pain in her heart had lifted.

She dragged the pile of branches out to the wood heap around the back and threw the weeds on to the compost heap.

'The right place for a certain person,' she muttered as

she briskly rubbed her hands to remove the last traces. She marched back to the garden to pick up the fork she had left behind in the garden—and stared.

Unsightly gaps in the frieze of the trees made her gasp. She hadn't realised the havoc she had wreaked. The trees held out mute stumpy ends to her.

'It's not fair,' she muttered as she wondered desperately how she could repair the damage.

'Oh, Stephanie!' The wail in her mother's voice as she came around the corner of the house told her that her work was as bad as she had feared.

'Sorry, Mum, I got carried away,' she apologised with genuine penitence.

'Never mind, dear, I was intending to give them a thorough pruning this year and for once I'm ahead of a job.'

'That's a brilliant recovery, Mum,' smiled Stephanie ruefully.

'Faster than the trees will make,' admitted her mother.

'I'll go and take a shower, maybe I should have had one before I started cutting!'

Stephanie was glad of the peace of her home that evening. No one had mentioned Dare, and as her brother had gone out earlier with a date the atmosphere was relaxed. The next day followed the usual Sunday routine of church and a picnic lunch. Stephanie had wondered how she would cope if Dare and his parents joined them, as had frequently occurred in the past, but although his parents did, Dare was absent.

She had always liked Dare's parents and she was surprised how quickly the afternoon passed. The long twilight meant she could stay until late in the evening, before driving along the flat plains, burnt almost sand-paper like by the sun.

Inside the flat the painting seemed more of a mockery than before. She found her eyes drawn to the picture of the Wellington flat's bedroom and the mirror with the word across it in scarlet. Her ears seemed to be filled with the word and she could almost feel Dare repulsing her again.

'I'll fix you!' she murmured.

She climbed gingerly on to a chair and reached for the picture cord. After a moment's effort she had the offending picture down.

'Now, what can I do with it?' she wondered out loud. The picture was too large to fit easily into any of her cupboards. In desperation she dragged it behind the sofa, but the frame showed over the top.

'At least the picture's out of sight,' she muttered. The wall seemed to laugh at her. The large empty space cried out for the vividness of colour.

'I'll replace it tomorrow,' Stephanie promised herself as she retired. 'And don't worry, Dare Nayton, I don't need you either!'

CHAPTER FOUR

'STEPHANIE? Mat here. I thought you might be interested to know that Ray's uncle is coming over to visit us on his latest picture hunt. I think he's probably good interview material. He's the one with the big London gallery.' Mat's telephone call had broken into her research time.

'That does sound promising. He's a world-rated authority on moderns, isn't he?'

'Yes, he's a well-known collector. I'll get Ray to drop in some of the details.'

'Splendid. How did the weekend go?'

'As weekends go, it went,' snorted Mat. 'I'm getting more grumpy than a grizzly bear in this heat. I swear Ray was thrilled to leave for work this morning.'

'You sound chirpy enough,' Stephanie commented.

'It's cooler today,' Mat explained.

'Come round for a meal tonight,' Stephanie invited.

'Stephanie, you're an angel! Ray and I would love that. I'd better check with him and ring you back.'

'That's fine. Maybe I'll see you later.'

Stephanie put down the phone. It wasn't like ebullient Mattie to be down in the dumps. She dismissed the thought as another phone call demanded her attention, and she found herself having to re-schedule a different appointment for a visiting dignitary. Only when Ray popped in later did she see that he too looked far from cheerful.

'Thanks for the invitation, Stephanie. We'll be there about seven, OK?'

'That's great, Ray.'

There was no time for further talk as her own programme was due to go on the air and she readied herself with the tapes for the technician and her lead-in notes. Once engrossed in the presentation she allowed nothing to distract her, and the red lights outside warned other staff of 'on air' operation. She had timed her presentation to the second and knew exactly when to begin her announcements, linking the tapes. When she did the final back announcement, she heard the theme music swell in her headphones and switched the microphone off gently. The red light went out and she saw the announcer in the next studio acknowledge her programme, although she couldn't hear what was said. She had already removed the headphones as soon as she had gone off mike. It took only a few seconds to straighten her papers and then she walked along to the technician at the control room.

She put a quick flick of her pen for those tapes she wanted erased as being of no further value and hesitated before the last one. The speaker had been good and she wondered if the person who had filled her position in Wellington would like it. She decided to submit it to Goldie, then he could pass it on as needed. She had two interviews scheduled for later in the day and she checked her files.

The first one was easy as a complete dossier had already been sent ahead by a publicity company with suggested angles and outlines. Stephanie admired the professional approach and contrasted it with the second interview, a local housewife who had won a major prize in the lottery.

Stephanie found the second a real challenge to her skill as the woman was so overcome with her news that every time she started speaking about the money she began to shake. It took time, but Stephanie finally succeeded and the interview turned out surprisingly well.

By the time she had finished Stephanie had to hurry to get to the fruiterers on her way home. It was next door to a cake shop and Stephanie looked admiringly at the confection of a gateau, thinking that Mattie had been the one who had always bought them in the past on gala occasions. She put it gingerly on to the front seat of her car and drove cautiously along the road to her flat. It had been fortunate that she had taken the car that morning as she didn't normally do so and without it she would have had a struggle to get everything home.

Hurriedly she changed and then prepared the meal so that everything would be ready before Mat and Ray arrived. Only as she set the table did she glance up to see the blank wall, and grimaced. Once again she had not bought a suitable painting, but she had no intention of putting the first back. In desperation her eyes lit on a bowl which she had picked up years before. It was a lovely piece and usually had pride of place in a cabinet. Now she took it out and placed it thoughtfully against the wall. The plainness of the spot showed off the lovely soft colours of the glaze, but she knew that by itself the ornament was too small. She had barely finished placing it when she heard Ray and Mat arrive.

'Stephanie, we're both looking forward to dinner. You always were such a great cook.'

'Hi, Stephanie, what happened to the painting?' Ray's artless question as he walked in showed that he had glanced straightaway to the wall. 'I really wanted to study that. I've been thinking about it.'

'I decided it was a bit hard to live with,' put in Stephanie with a wry grimace. She tried to pretend she didn't see the warning nudge Mat had sent to her husband.

'I'll put on the steaks, I've got them marinating.'

Because she had done so much earlier it took little preparation. She didn't even have to ask how they liked their steaks, as she knew exactly. When they sat down to eat the atmosphere was lighthearted and by the time they were ready to devour the exotic, much admired gateau, Stephanie could sense none of the despondency of the morning.

'Stephanie, you're a real pal,' smiled Mat. 'I was so down in the dumps! You see, Ray's been told there's a possibility of a transfer. That's the crux of the problem. We're happy here, we've made friends, we've got our dear little flat, and I don't want to move.'

'It's not certain, just a grapevine rumour that a vacancy is coming up, and it could improve my grade,' Ray explained.

'Mat, it's not like you to worry over a situation until it arises. It may be back in Timaru, where you came from originally.'

'Not with my luck,' put in Mat. 'The family would turn cartwheels if that happened!'

'The list of vacancies will be out on Monday week, why don't you stop worrying and wait and see. After all, you don't have to go,' said Stephanie.

'Just what I've been trying to tell you, Matilda,' smiled Ray. Stephanie waited for the explosion of wrath from the use of the full name, but she knew her friend was upset when she let it pass unchallenged.

'Let's talk about the baby. Have you decided upon a name?' Stephanie noted with relief that both Ray and Mat cheered up immediately. When they left it was quite late, and she found herself strangely lonely.

Her fingers tapped along the edge of the sofa and hit the hard frame of the picture. She drew back suddenly and a small splinter on the back of the frame went into her finger.

'Typical!' she groaned as she reached into a sewing basket for a needle. 'Dare can hurt me without even trying!'

To her annoyance the splinter had gone in at a bad angle, and having to use her left hand made it difficult. She finally succeeded in extricating the offending piece of woodwork with a sigh of relief, and wished she could remove a certain man from her thoughts just as readily.

Stephanie started the week in a flurry of reports; it helped her keep her mind on work, and those times that she did find herself puzzling over the incident with Dare, she hastily banished the thought. She went out one evening with a group of other staff to see a play and was asked out by a new member of the copy department, who had just arrived from Auckland. The party was a small one but enormous fun. Her escort was witty and Stephanie found herself liking his company, and she knew her escort was enjoying himself too. Even so, when he asked her for a date on the Saturday night, she was quick to tell him that she went home most weekends.

Afterwards she wondered why she had been so anxious

to keep their relationship on a platonic level. Nevertheless her hasty explanation meant that she would have to go home that weekend. She took the car to work on Friday and drove straight home after work.

All the way home she kept wondering if Dare would be there, swimming in the pool, when she arrived. It was almost an anticlimax to find that Alan and Dare had gone to town earlier and were not expected back until much later. She enjoyed relaxing with her parents, catching up on the latest news and hearing about the thousand and one things to do with the farm.

The clock striking nine-thirty told her that the boys would be arriving from town, and as Dare usually came in for supper with Alan she decided to avoid a confrontation by going to bed early. She had barely reached her bedroom when she heard the car stop and a second later heard Dare's voice.

'No, I won't come in tonight, thanks, Alan. I'll see you tomorrow.'

The car powered away and Stephanie relaxed, realising with a smile that all her muscles in her stomach had been tight with tension. She began to wonder if Dare had deliberately stayed away because she was at home. Alan would have mentioned it and he would have been reminded by the presence of her car. She tossed in the bed, regretting her self-imposed early night and planning a way to avoid Dare if he called the next day.

Her problem was solved as the men were all busy at Naytons' haymaking. She had been quite content to do extra baking and run it up to Aunt Olivia and see the pleasure on Dare's mother's face. She kept Stephanie entertained with tales that Dare had told them of life overseas. As the hay paddock was close to the house the men did not need the smoko carted out to them, so Stephanie made sure she set the table ready before disappearing back down the drive.

The chestnut trees lining the drive were already losing some of the spiky balls and she bent down to pick up one of the nuts. Its colour was deep reddish brown and it gleamed after a quick rub against her sleeve. The whorl of the grain was an unusual marking and she viewed it carefully, remembering that it had been Dare who had first drawn her attention to the individuality of the grain marks. Dare had spent hours sketching the trees, and the flowers in his drawings in their delicate pink and white beauty had reminded her of tiny orchids, or if they were still upright on the branch, like a miniature Christmas tree lit with candles. Absently Stephanie rubbed the nut again. As children they had had wonderful games with them, juggling them and throwing them at targets like fence posts.

'You look a little dangerous—you weren't intending to throw it at anyone, I hope?'

The mocking voice startled her and she glanced up to see Dare approaching.

'I thought you'd be hard at work with the haymaking. Gone soft overseas?' she jeered.

He shot her a dark brooding glance.

'You know better than that.' His voice had gone cold and Stephanie wished she had not been quite so hasty in throwing down the gauntlet. She realised then that the harvester that had been a constant noise in the background had stopped.

'Have you finished?' she asked in surprise.

'Mechanical failure.'

Stephanie felt small. She could see now that Dare was carrying a metal part and she wished she had noticed it at the beginning. He had always been good at fixing mechanical things and she guessed that he had offered to do the job while the others had a well-earned rest.

'If you're not busy I could do with a hand.'

Dare spoke crisply and she turned and followed meekly as he led the way down a side path to the toolshed, beside the woolshed. Stephanie gazed around at the neat racks of equipment and work benches that had been a familiar sight in past years. She wondered when she had last been in the shed and guessed it would have been when she was about fifteen.

Dare sorted out some small pieces and set a machine into action. He seemed totally unaware that she was still standing there as he concentrated on the job in hand. Stephanie grinned, thinking that at the moment at least they were not fighting with each other. Her eyes flicked down to Dare's hands as he guided the piece. With a start she realised that she was supposed to assist and she looked carefully at the problem, before putting her hand beside Dare's. Concentration was difficult; she was overwhelmingly conscious of him leaning forward beside her, his muscles taut. Somehow she gathered her thoughts and worked smoothly, feeding in the piece at the right angle.

'That should do it.'

Dare's voice sounded cool to her sensitive ear. He lifted the shining metal and switched the machine off. For a moment she watched as he rubbed the fine dust away and then selected another piece. She noted that his judgment was as sharp as ever. The piece had been honed to perfection and fitted neatly into place.

He flicked the main power supply off and turned to shut the door after her. Stephanie stood still, remembering the last time he had held her in his arms when he had opened the door at the studio. She knew her breathing was rapid, but she deliberately looked away. Instinctively, she felt Dare was aware of the tension too. With a great effort she stepped forward, apparently calmly towards the drive.

'Thanks, Stephanie.'

She nodded, not willing to trust herself to speak. When she reached the drive again she raced back towards her own home. Her heart was thumping painfully and she wondered with a feeling of desperation why Dare could affect her so badly, simply by his mere presence.

'He doesn't even like me,' she told herself, as she finally slowed down once the boundary fence was in sight. Behind her the steady thrum of the harvester had begun again, and she twisted her mouth wryly at the thought that Dare could even make the wretched machine run smoothly. It wouldn't dare to break down again!

'Ah, there you are, Stephanie.' Her mother smiled and stopped her weeding in the garden. 'I've just put the kettle on, would you like to make the tea?'

'Of course.' Stephanie smiled at her mother, glad to switch her mind from their next-door neighbour.

'Your garden's looking really pretty, Mum. Those pink dahlias mix well with the pink begonias. Even the trees on that side don't look nearly so bad as last week.'

'Yes, it's coming along quite well. I must admit Dare made a marvellous job of pruning and shaping the branches for me. He spent hours on it last week. Wasn't it thoughtful of him? It's such a pleasure having him home again.'

'I'll make the tea.' Stephanie stalked off to the kitchen, her heels beating an angry march. 'Trust Mr Marvellous,' she muttered. 'I ruin the trees and he saves the situation!'

She took the cups and teapot out to the garden and put them on the outdoor table, turning her chair so she would not have to look at the trees Dare had cleverly trimmed.

Pouring the tea, she realised that since Dare had returned, her even life had been thrown into emotional havoc. Everything seemed to be associated with the wretched man. Even a simple thing like pouring tea. What had he said . . . 'Patron of the right things brigade'. Her anger simmered and she almost scalded herself taking a mouthful of the boiling liquid.

'You look a trifle flushed, dear. Are you sure you're not working too hard?' Her mother looked concerned. Stephanie hastily reassured her.

'Mum, I've had a very easy week. However, next week I might stay in town at the weekend.'

'Well, I'm glad you could come home this weekend. We're going up to the bush for a picnic tomorrow. Olivia suggested it yesterday.'

'To the bush?' Stephanie queried. Her thoughts began flying as she wondered how she could possibly extricate herself from the picnic. Dare had always loved the small patch of bush that was at the far end of the farm. Her thoughts flicked back to four years before. They had gone riding together and had raced each other to the bush. Dare had helped her down and together they had wandered through the trees, stopping to kiss frequently, delighting in being together. Dare had led her to the totara tree, the slow-growing forest giant. He had pulled out his small sketch pad and pencil. She had laid back on the grass content, as his hand moved the pencil over the page. With eyes full of love she had turned to him as he handed her the sketch.

'To the girl I intend to marry,' he had written neatly at the top. It was a drawing of the totara tree and he had drawn two figures at the base.

'For ever and a day, my love,' he had said quietly as she looked at him. She had held out her arms and he had kissed her with such tenderness, she thought it strange the world should remain the same.

She looked around at the totara tree and their surroundings.

'You know the story of the totara wood, my love?' Dare had whispered, his voice gentle in her ear. At her questioning glance he explained.

'The old Maori people admired the kauri, the great tall hardwood tree and spoke of it as the tree that lasts for ever.' His smile was sweet. 'But of the totara they say it lasts for ever and a day. That's how long my love will last.'

'For ever and a day,' Stephanie said softly, melting in Dare's embrace.

'Stephanie—Stephanie, you must be miles away!'

With a start Stephanie realised that her mother was standing staring at her.

'Sorry, Mum, I was just thinking about something.' She realised that her mother was holding a large container full of potatoes and moved rapidly forward to take it.

'I thought I'd make an extra large amount of potato salad for the picnic. It's always popular.'

As Stephanie rubbed the dirt from the newly dug

potatoes she realised that she had come down to earth in more ways than one. Thinking about the idyllic scene in the bush was too painful, and she had never revisited the spot since. As she scrubbed the peel off she wondered with a quiet desperation how she could avoid the picnic. She knew she could not sit and be polite in front of Dare, wondering if he was remembering their truth of four years before. His words 'For ever and a day' mocked her. His love hadn't lasted once she was out of sight, she thought bitterly.

She plopped a potato into the pot of water and the splash sent a drop of water on to her face. It ran down her cheek like a tear. Her days of crying over Dare had finished, she reminded herself. She was not going to allow herself to become emotionally involved again. If it was possible she would avoid the next day's picnic at the bush, if not she would just have to see how strong she could be. After all, she reminded herself, facing up to the very spot might have a beneficial effect, she could discover it meant nothing at all.

'I think we might take the truck up to the valley.'

Stephanie heard her father explain to Dare as they stood outside church on Sunday.

'It would be a lot easier than carting all the food by hand. We could leave the truck at the edge of the bush and set up a barbecue farther in. If I remember right there used to be a small clearing in by the giant totara tree.'

Stephanie was aware of Dare's glance resting for a fraction of a second on her face. She tried to keep nonchalant, telling herself that she was a fool to care.

'I wish I'd known you were planning to go there. There's a wasp's nest right by that area. If I'd realised I could have cleared it earlier. I'm sorry, but I think we'd better pick somewhere else. Could I suggest Birdlings Flat? You'd be able to put the fishing gear in too,' Dare grinned.

'Capital suggestion—a bit of luck you knew about the wasps. I think everyone will think the beach is a good substitute.'

Stephanie turned away, relieved that at least one memory would remain intact. Her father would be delighted to play at being a fisherman. As small children they had spent many hours on that particular piece of coast. Alan and Dare had enjoyed the fishing, but after the first piteous glance at the dying fish, she had declared herself more interested in the stones on the beach. Nothing would make her pick up a rod again.

Her collection of stones had grown impressively as the Birdlings Flat area was known internationally to rock hounds. Although the beach was not suitable for swimming she had always managed to get wet, lured further into the water by the shininess of a particular pebble. Some of the times she had been able to beat the waves with her fist closed over a particular stone, but at other times the waves crashed over her legs just as she was about to grasp the pebble.

'We'll meet you down there.'

The words drifted towards her, Dare standing tall beside Alan.

'I might take my gear out. I unpacked the portable easel in the last crate during the week. I haven't had much time to think about painting lately.'

'Be a change from haymaking,' laughed Alan. 'Stephanie, are you going to add to your collection of rocks?'

'Probably,' Stephanie conceded with a lightness she was far from feeling. 'I haven't been down to Birdlings Flat for years.'

'I'll be a little late arriving, I told Barbara I'd pick her up after lunch,' said Dare.

Stephanie felt a shiver run through her. He had said the name with such ease it was almost as if his girl-friend's presence would be taken for granted.

She was glad that she was approached by one of their other neighbours at the time. It was only polite to excuse herself and talk to the couple who had approached her. To her relief Dare had already disappeared when she glanced round again. She guessed he would have lunch in town with Barbara before bringing her out to the beach.

'Barbara's really terrific,' Alan told her.

Stephanie hid a wince at the words. Somehow she had managed to forget about Barbara.

'What's she look like?' she asked airily.

'A doll! Blonde, blue eyes, a figure that's all curves in all the right places,' Alan informed her with a twinkle in his eyes.

'You're having me on.'

'Wait and see,' he responded.

'Brothers!' Stephanie tossed at him as she walked towards the car.

The beach was almost hidden by the hills of shingle and after helping carry the picnic seats, rugs and cushions Stephanie wandered over towards the sea. The waves raised in blue-green clarity to a roll, which curved to a screaming white crash as they approached the beach.

There was a fascination that never failed for Stephanie and she stood, just watching it, only vaguely aware of the outlines of her father and brother already setting up their fishing rods. A number of other fishermen were standing patiently, their absorbed attention making them seem in tune with the sea and sky. Even as she looked along the line of the beach she saw a flash of silver as a fish was landed.

Hastily she looked down at her feet, scrunching the tiny pebbles with her toes. Taking care to avoid the spaces of the sportsmen, she followed the colours of the stones. At first sight they all appeared grey or brown, but closer inspection revealed a myriad colours. Scooping up a handful, she studied them carefully; the majority were the soft grey, but then she selected a deep purple, a marbled green and white, and a stone seemingly made up of a composite of coloured flecks. She put the last three into a plastic bag and sitting down on the stones began picking over more of the treasure.

'Lunch, Stephanie!'

The command broke into her thoughts and she discarded most of the stones in her hand. Gradually she had walked away from her family. She looked at the group with love. It was good to be home and to be with her family, and particularly good that she didn't have to sit and try to be polite in front of a certain man. Already she had decided to go fossicking further along the beach later, to ensure a healthy distance between the precious Barbara and the arrogant Dare, and herself.

The sea air had given them all healthy appetites and there was a great deal of chatter and laughter over the meal. Stephanie displayed the stones she had gathered and Dare's mother admired a very unusual soft dusky pink stone with a zigzag design in white.

'This is lovely, Stephanie. It's just the colour of my new dress.'

'I'll make it up for you,' Stephanie promised. 'Would you like it as a drop style like a fob or set into a brooch?'

'It's such an unusual one it should be shown off as a fob style, I think.'

'I wonder what type of stone it is?'

'Dare would know,' commented Alan as he handed it back to her.

Stephanie nodded. Dare would know, she thought sourly. He would be able to identify the stones as readily as a child knows the whereabouts of the biscuit tin.

'I'll help you clear away.' Stephanie suited action to the words to the howl of protest from her father, who decided he wasn't so anxious to move. Amid laughter as she tipped him out the rest was swiftly packed away. Her mother and Olivia Nayton declared themselves on strike and watched as the rest of the family tidied the area. Both ladies settled back to snooze and chatter idly. Stephanie, after a glance at her watch, decided she would begin her meandering way across the beach. The desolate harshness of the area seemed to be right for her mood.

Seagulls screamed abuse at her as she walked further towards the edge of the beach. Glancing back, she could just make out the figures of her father and even as she looked she saw two people approach him. She knew instinctively that Dare was introducing the 'smashing' Barbara, and a minute later they were joined by Alan and Dare's father. Stooping down to pick up another stone, she wondered at her own curiosity. Deliberately she moved behind the curve of the beach so that she could not be seen.

'Admit it, Stephanie, Dare still holds some attraction for you,' she told herself sadly. 'And you're jealous. But Dare isn't interested in you, and the faster you're sensible about it the better off you'll be.'

She threw the handful of stones at the empty beach. A red-beaked gull looked at her with coolly assessing eyes, its white-grey plumage immaculate. Every smooth feather was tucked so perfectly into place that in its stillness it seemed like a statue. Only the bright scarlet legs contrasted with its snow soft feathers.

'You're beautiful,' Stephanie told the bird. 'If Dare were here he'd sketch you.' The bird solemnly turned and preened itself, then satisfied, it regarded her with a more quizzical expression.

'Sorry, I haven't any food with me. Later on there'll be more, if I know my family.'

Lazily the gull opened its wings and ran forward a few steps before launching itself into the air. For a few moments its shape was a perfect aerodynamic silhouette against the blue of the sky. Stephanie followed its path and found it leading her between scrubby grass and lupins back to the settlement of baches which people used mostly as holiday homes. She picked an isolated section and leant against a small shrub. The soft sound of the sea in the distance and the summer sun made her feel relaxed.

The seagull had long disappeared and Stephanie shut her eyes against the brightness of the sky. A faint rustle immediately above her ear made her roll over in haste. She smiled, seeing her 'creepy-crawlie' was a tiny temple-like chrysalis and the butterfly was about to emerge.

Fascinated, she watched with absorbed attention as it appeared, its body seeming to swell as it reached out with its long legs.

Another sound made her turn her head and she saw Dare watching her. To her surprise he was alone. Heart thumping, she hid her feelings by turning back to watch the tiny creature as it gained a foothold onto the small branch. Dare sat down beside her, his eyes also on the butterfly.

'A Monarch,' he said softly. 'Mind if I join you?'

Stephanie did mind. She minded with every single part of her body, but with Dare Nayton already seated beside her, she was too breathless to answer.

CHAPTER FIVE

DARE had already pulled out his sketch block and his pencil moved rapidly. Already the atmosphere was totally different. Dare's long tanned muscular legs were touching her own. Stephanie sat up swiftly, but kept her eyes on the butterfly.

'Take your time, little lady, a bug doesn't turn into a butterfly easily,' Dare commented quietly.

'A bug doesn't turn into a butterfly!' hissed Stephanie crossly.

Dare gave her an enigmatic look. 'Are you sure?'

She knew her pulses were tingling. It wasn't fair, she thought, that Dare had so much magnetism. She forced herself to look away.

'Oh, look!' The words were drawn from her in enchantment. The former drab bundle of tissue on the creature's back had been pumped full of life and the wings, even as they watched, took shape and colour. With a slow motion the butterfly opened and shut them experimentally and they had a glimpse of bright orange criss-crossed with black.

'It's like the lead work on a stained glass window, with the sun on it,' she said.

Dare's pencil flew faster as the monarch wavered its wings uncertainly. The small creature must have worked some magic, as there was harmony between Stephanie and Dare as they shared the miracle.

Again the butterfly moved and this time the strength of its action was responsible for lifting it off the branch. Stephanie and Dare both laughed in delight as it regained its perch, obviously surprised. Its recovery time was almost immediate as it fluttered forward, then bravely decided to launch out. The first flight was a short affair and all three shared the thrill of the moment. Landing again on a lower branch with an anxious fluttering of its wings, it seemed to survey its new world, inspecting both of them, its feelers finely tuned. Evidently it decided the world was fascinating as it lifted itself and fluttered off, its wings flashing orange and black against the blue of the sky.

Dare bent to his sketching and Stephanie silently watched, noting the rapidity of his movement and the carefully precise detail. He had captured the delicacy of the butterfly as its head and long legs emerged and in another its first efforts to pump its wings upright. A third sketch showed the wing detail and a fourth was mainly of its body which Stephanie had scarcely noticed as she had been so engrossed with its wings.

'Want to look?' Dare offered. She studied the page carefully.

'It's good,' she commented at last.

His lips curved into a hint of a smile and the blue eyes danced. Instead of speaking he began sketching again, and Stephanie wished she could see. In a few moments he slipped the sheet out and handed it to her. A large butterfly with wings upraised perched perilously on a twiggy branch. Its body was different in that it had been changed to resemble her; two long slim legs and arms featured. The eyes captured her attention and she knew that if Dare had used colour they would have been her own ginger ones, as Dare had drawn her head instead of the butterfly's.

'To a little bug that grew into a beautiful butterfly, my apologies,' Stephanie read.

She looked at Dare and felt her body quicken. Slowly he put down the sketch pad, his movements deliberate. Stephanie moistened her lips, knowing that he wanted to kiss her. Was it just as obvious, she wondered, that she desperately wanted his touch too?

Almost shyly her eyes met his.

'You're a butterfly, Stephanie, an exotic, fascinating creature sipping delight and giving pleasure from man to man,' he whispered.

His mouth hovered above hers for a moment, then he kissed her, his hands holding her pinned on the ground.

'I'm just as susceptible as your other men, Stephanie,' Dare murmured as he took her mouth again. The lean hardness of his body held her imprisoned. Agonised by his words, she tried to struggle, forcing her hands to push him away, despite the attraction that had flared between them.

'Such a display!' he mocked, releasing her. 'Who are you trying to impress? I'm not some callow youth in love with you.'

'You're hateful, Dare Nayton!' Giant sobs racked Stephanie, her body trembling as she sat up.

'Your apology is an insult.' Ripping the sketch to pieces, she flung it at him, then stood up and ran toward the beach. Her thoughts were in a turmoil as she stopped to catch her breath once she was out of Dare's sight. A handy log was in front of her and she sat down and thrust her face despairingly into her hands.

Dare's words hung mockingly in the air . . . '. . . You're a butterfly . . . giving delight from man to man . . . such a display . . . I'm not some callow youth in love with you'. The hurtful phrases stung. He could not have taunted her in a more damaging way, she decided, and the very knowledge helped her, as she felt anger rise to prevent the tears.

Only then did she wonder where his girl-friend was, if Dare was alone. A moment's thought told her that he had probably wandered away along to do his sketching. It had been a trick of fate that he had found her in all the wilderness. Like the waves crashing on the beach, their feelings had the certainty of the inevitable. Sighing, she made her way back to the beach, slowly, stopping to pick up more pebbles on the way.

'Hey, Sis, come and meet Barbara!'

Her brother had evidently been coaching the girl in holding the rod and casting the line. His smile was wide and admiring as he looked at the girl. Stephanie forced herself forward.

'My brother told me you were a real smasher,' she smiled, 'and I can see he's right.'

She found herself able to smile at the girl. Barbara had a lovely warmth and the introductions passed more easily than Stephanie had thought possible.

'I've heard of you from Dare, of course, and I've heard you on the radio. It's fun to put a face to the voice.'

'And I've seen some of your work in pottery,' said Stephanie. 'You're very talented.'

'Not really. I enjoy puddling, but I'm not disciplined

enough to make a real potter,' the girl answered regretfully. 'There's too many wonderful things to do. Your
brother's teaching me to fish, whereas Dare will be away
sketching. That's the difference, of course!' she laughed
gaily. 'Dare's an artist, I'm a hobbyist.'

'And there's nothing wrong with that,' put in Alan.
'When you provide such a picture of beauty, you don't
have to be anything.'

'Alan, you're a flatterer.' The blonde curls danced in
the sunlight. 'Stephanie, watch me.' With remarkable
skill Barbara cast her line, while Alan watched approving-
ly. Stephanie, glancing at her brother, knew a stab of
concern. She had never seen him so obviously smitten by
any girl.

Barbara leaned against Alan as he corrected her arm
position and glanced flirtatiously up at him with her deep
blue eyes, her mouth a wide curve. She turned back to
Stephanie, including her in the admirer's gallery.

'How's that?'

Stephanie smiled acknowledgment, then glanced down
at her feet. Two of the same unusual dusky pink and white
stones lay together. She picked them up quickly and
added them to her collection.

'There you are, Stephanie, you've missed out on afternoon tea.'

Aunt Olivia and her mother had abandoned their deck
chairs and approached the group.

'It doesn't matter, I'm not hungry,' put in Stephanie.
'A little thirsty, I think.'

'There's a little tea left if you like to help yourself. We
should be starting for home shortly. Are you going back to
town tonight or will you drive in tomorrow?'

'I'll go back tonight, then I have a straight run in the morning—I've got a busy day tomorrow.'

Stephanie was glad to be avoiding any more scenes. She wished she had taken her own car, she would have loved to have driven away immediately from any possibility of any encounter with Dare. A pulse at her temple throbbed at the thought.

'I'll get some tea,' she excused herself hastily.

Her feet slithered as she scrambled over the pile of stones to the car, where she found the tea was still piping hot in the flask.

'Any left?' queried a deep male voice.

'A little, Dare,' she answered coolly with a calm she didn't feel. She put down the flask in front of him so he could help himself, after she had poured one for herself. With a grin for her attitude he reached past her for a clean mug. Stephanie tried not to show her chagrin, realising that she would have been a lot better off if she could have been polite and poured him one too. At least then he would have had no excuse to keep his arm across her, as he deliberated aloud on whether he wanted a brown mug or a beige one.

In self-defence Stephanie reached out, grabbed one of the mugs, poured tea into it and handed it to him.

'You do that so graciously,' he murmured, his eyes dancing.

He knew she was furious with him, she thought crossly. She gulped a mouthful of the tea she had poured for herself, but with the delay it had gone cool.

'You can share mine,' Dare offered mockingly, seeing her moue of distaste.

'This is fine,' Stephanie said shortly.

'Easily pleased,' commented Dare.

His words grated. She knew the innuendo he was implying. She felt tears spring to her eyes and her throat seemed oddly tense.

'Dare, stop it. I can't go on fighting.'

Facing him, she saw him study her closely and his eyes softened.

'I'm sorry, Stephanie.'

He put down the mug and strode away leaving her feelings more mixed than before. Dare's apology had been genuine, Stephanie conceded. She brushed the traces of tears away and repacked the flask and the mugs. With infinite relief she saw her father heading towards the car and realised that her mother's intention to reach home early was to be satisfied.

She was glad that her father was so overjoyed with the results of his fishing expedition that he didn't notice her own silence. Several red cod attested to the day's skill, and Alan had successfully landed a greyboy, a four-foot-long shark.

'Barbara caught a spiny dogfish,' announced Alan, sounding more proud of the girl's despised catch than his own.

Barbara had caught more than that, thought Stephanie. Yet why had Dare deliberately set out to look for her that afternoon?

'This is Stephanie Fernley of Radio Three WS saying "Good Morning".' Stephanie switched her microphone off, stepping out of the chair while her theme played. The announcer slipped in and turned on the microphone.

'Thank you, Stephanie, and a reminder that Local

Scene with more news and views of the region will be on the air again on Wednesday morning.' He began spinning a disc and reached for a copy commercial. His microphone light went out and he turned to Stephanie.

'Any chance of you doing a shift for me, Stephanie? I've got the Saturday night shift again and—hold it . . .' He flicked on the microphone, read with convincing enthusiasm the delights of wearing jeans by a certain manufacturer, announced the next record and flicked the control for the next disc. The red light faded and he continued in his conversation '. . . so if you could help, I know the boss will OK it. I've been invited to take part in a hang glider contest up North and I won't be back in time. Ray will be doing the programme,' he added, as the gentleman concerned appeared, to deposit some more tapes, discs and logs in the studio.

'I deny all knowledge of everything,' said Ray with an easy grin. 'Stephanie, you were right, Timaru is on offer.'

'Go to it!' Stephanie smiled, remembering Mat and Ray's discussion of a possible transfer. 'I'll do the shift,' she told the announcer.

He signalled a commercial and Stephanie fled the studio before the red light demanded silence again. Going straight to her office, she noted the times in her schedule for the Saturday. She knew the diary's entry for that day would be a blank. There was also a bonus in providing an excuse not to go home that weekend. As she put her diary back in its usual pigeonhole, she looked up to see Ray had followed her.

'I've rung Mat,' he said, 'Of course, I might not get the promotion, but on the other hand . . .'

'I'm sure you'd stand a first-rate chance. I like your

programmes, Ray, and I'll miss you when you go to Timaru. Mat will be thrilled, though, and it will be lovely for the family with the new baby.'

'Steady on, I haven't even applied yet!' Ray grinned lightheartedly. 'Tell me what I should put.'

'Ask Mat,' chuckled Stephanie. 'What about coming for dinner tonight? Dad caught some red cod yesterday and he seems to have given me a pile of fillets.'

'Love to, and I know Mat won't need a second invitation. Give her a ring and see if it's all right with her. By the way, that uncle of mine is due on Thursday. He's advanced his schedule so he can have longer here.'

Again Stephanie made a note on her desk diary and even as she rang Mat she pulled out the impressive file of notes which Ray had given her the week before. Evidently the relative's reputation as a collector and gallery owner was well justified. Over dinner they discussed the timing of the interview, and in order to make things easier Stephanie suggested that they call in for coffee on the way back from the airport and do the interview at the same time.

On Wednesday, she left work earlier than usual with her tape recorder and microphone. Once home she scurried round cleaning the flat, then arranged fresh flowers. The long blank wall still bothered her, as did the picture frame sticking up at the back of the sofa.

'Well, Dare Nayton, you did apologise,' she muttered as she balanced precariously, struggling to rehang the picture.

'That's better,' she told herself. The picture fitted the room so well she knew that it was the reason she had not been able to find anything else she liked. She looked at the clock and put on the coffee percolator. The aroma of freshly brewed coffee was just beginning to waft into the room when the door bell pealed.

Introductions over, she led the way into the lounge.

'I'll make the coffee immediately and we can discuss the interview while we have a drink,' she explained.

Ray and Mat seated themselves and Stephanie prepared to go through to the kitchen, when she noticed Mr Walker, the director, staring at Dare's painting.

'Fascinating—it must be a Nayton. I met him in France two years ago, then he sold me some of his work when he returned to London. This isn't his usual type of painting, yet the technique is almost identical.'

He turned to Stephanie with an enquiring glance.

'It is by Dare Nayton,' she confessed. 'Painted four years ago.'

'Let me know if ever you want to sell it,' he commented, his tone appreciative. 'I hope to purchase more while I'm here.'

Stephanie fled to make the drinks; she didn't want to face any more questions until she had regained her composure. She was relieved when she carried in the tray to see that Mat and Ray were entertaining Mr Walker.

She outlined the interview and they had just finished it when the doorbell rang. She left Mat and Ray to discuss painting with their visitor and went slowly, to the door wondering who it would be.

'Aunt Olivia, this is a surprise!' she exclaimed.

'I was visiting a friend of mine in hospital and I thought I'd call in while I was passing. I can see you have visitors, dear, I'll pop in another time.' She began to move away, but Stephanie took her arm.

'Nonsense, I'm delighted you decided to visit. I want you to meet Mat and Ray. I flatted with Mat in Wellington, you may remember. Their uncle is a director of a gallery in London. He bought some of Dare's work overseas.'

'What a coincidence!'

'I'd very much like to see some more of your son's work,' commented Mr Walker, when the introductions had been made.

'Why not come out tomorrow? Stephanie could bring you tomorrow night. Stay for dinner and I can show you some of Dare's early work. Not that I intend parting with it.'

Stephanie's brows creased into a frown at the invitation. She couldn't imagine anything worse than to have to face Dare again and sit opposite him at dinner.

'I'll have to check with my nephew and his wife, they may have something planned,' he said.

'Why not come too?' asked Mrs Nayton, smiling at Mat and Ray.

'I'd like to, but it's our last ante-natal meeting,' put in Mat. 'We were wondering how we could entertain Uncle at the same time.'

'Then it's settled. Stephanie will drive your uncle out as soon as she is finished work.'

Weakly Stephanie nodded assent, then turned to the coffee pot to hide her feelings.

After her guests had left Stephanie made herself sit down and annotate the interview. The name of Dare Nayton was mentioned among the new artists of international stature, and Stephanie began to have some idea of Dare's prestige overseas. It began to explain the new studio and apartment he had designed. Typically Dare had scarcely mentioned his success. Her eyes went to the painting on the wall, she wondered what the director would have thought if he knew she had stowed it away behind the sofa most of the time. The thought brought a smile back to her eyes until she remembered that the following day the Naytons would expect her to bring the director out to the farm.

She wondered if it was possible to ring her Aunt Olivia and explain that she felt it better to drop Mr Walker and pick him up afterwards. With a wry twist of her lips she shook her head. Aunt Olivia would be hurt if she took that way out. Besides, by now Dare would have been told, and she could imagine his raised brows if she sought an excuse. At least, she thought, Dare's parents would be there all the time, and Mr Walker. She would regard it as a work situation and be calm and professional and totally ignore any feelings for Dare Nayton.

'What a beautiful setting!'

Mr Walker's enthusiastic comment as they pulled up outside the Naytons' farmhouse made Stephanie look around her with new eyes. The drive of the chestnut trees had grown to magnificent height and formed a gold and green backdrop to the sand-coloured plains. A section of the farm which was under cultivation showed almost black green in sharp contrast, as the sun was low in the sky and the hills of Banks Peninsula appeared almost sculptured into position behind them; Stephanie guided her car to a standstill, and even as they opened the doors Olivia Nayton came out to greet them.

'Stephanie, you show the way to the studio, dear, I'm

sure Dare will prefer to show you the work he's doing at the moment. Later I could show you the sketches I kept. Stephanie has some of her own, of course, I believe she was Dare's usual subject when she was younger.'

'Along with sheep, dogs and the horses,' put in Stephanie self-mockingly. Sighing inwardly, she led the way down the familiar brick path. Mr Walker looked about him with keenly observant eyes.

'This is a bonus I didn't expect. To be honest, I didn't know where to find Nayton. The last few years he's spent quite a time on the Continent. I remember him telling me one day that this was his home, but somehow I had the impression that he didn't intend to return.'

'I think his parents thought four years was quite a long time.'

'But not you?' questioned the director with a smile.

Stephanie avoided the question. 'That's the studio, ahead. It used to be a barn and Dare had it converted. I don't want to intrude, so I'll leave you now.'

With relief she turned back towards the farmhouse, only to walk straight into Dare who had approached from a side path. His hands gripped her arms to steady her and she was immediately aware of the magnetism which arrowed between them.

'Running away, Stephanie?' Dare's eyes gleamed as he turned her around. 'In order to get your commission you have to be present at the sale.'

'What are you talking about?' Stephanie asked warily.

'Come on, we'd better not keep the man waiting,' he said. He tugged her along, his hand closed firmly on hers.

Willy-nilly, Stephanie found herself back at the studio. The doors were opened wide and Mr Walker had already entered, his figure still against the canvas in front of him.

'Oh, no!' Stephanie felt the impact of the painting like a sudden thrust of pain.

Even in the evening light the painting glowed vibrantly, showing the wings of the butterfly spread in almost translucent beauty. Like the quick sketch that Dare had given her, which she had ripped in two, the body of the butterfly was a girl's body with a hint of languor about its pose.

'It's brilliant!' announced the director, after shaking hands with Dare. 'I want it, of course.'

'Sorry, it's not for sale.' Dare's voice was quiet and Stephanie swallowed quickly, feeling the muscles tense in her throat. Even though the girl was not recognisable as a portrait she knew Dare had modelled it on her. Dare had deliberately forced her to the studio so she would see the painting, she realised. Determined not to lose her composure, she spoke thoughtfully as though analysing the work.

'Do you really like it?' She turned to Mr Walker. 'Personally, I think it's overdone—it's too vivid, too unreal.'

'Ah, but my dear Miss Fernley, that's where the subtlety enters. I think your friend is forcing the point home more effectively by that very exaggeration. Its barren surroundings all contribute to the impact. It's good, very, very good.'

Stephanie met Dare's eyes as he challenged her to make another derogatory comment. With chagrin she turned away to hide the feelings which burnt through her.

She studiously avoided looking at the two men and walked over to sit on the sheepskin mat at the other end of the room. There she could observe the painting from a distance and she had to admit to herself that it was a remarkable study. If it did not have such hidden meaning for her she would have been as impressed as the director.

'I haven't had time to work on very much since I've been home. I've been rather busy setting up the studio. However, I have a couple of small canvases you could be interested in.'

Dare's voice sounded even as he approached and pulled out a rack. He clipped one board into position and flicked the lights. Instantly the landscape reflecting the heat of a nor'-west day on the plains came into focus. The ground looked barren and burnt almost to a stubble.

'The second is in the same theme, Earth and Sky,' commented Dare as he adjusted the lights again, after placing another picture into position.

Stephanie, despite her feelings over Dare's painting of the butterfly, was impressed. Like twin images reversed, the sky's patterns of clouds seemed to echo the sculptured land forms.

'These are for sale,' commented Dare. 'Specially for you!'

'I'll take both of them,' said Mr Walker quickly.

Stephanie saw her opportunity to slip away as Dare reached down the painting of the sky. Slowly she walked back to the gate which separated the home paddock. The orange of the butterfly seemed to have filled the sky with the sunset. Even as she watched the colour flared into apricots and pinks before turning deep purple with the approach of night. She watched the beautiful display, heedless of time.

'Waiting for me?' queried Dare, a mocking note in his

voice. He joined her, leaning nonchalantly against the gate. His eyes scanned the horizon briefly before resting on her face.

'Where's Mr Walker?' asked Stephanie, trying to show she was not affected by presence and reminding herself that she was to be calm.

'Gone for a walk; he wanted to have a look around while there's still a small amount of light. He'll be back in a few moments. I'd better get changed.'

Stephanie glanced down at the casual shorts Dare was wearing. The long muscular legs were deeply tanned and looked strong and lithe. Catching her glance, he grinned at her and his hand flicked gently against the line of her chin. Discomfited, Stephanie glared at him then remembered her resolution and turned away.

'I'll go and help your mother.'

'Coward!' Dare's voice taunted as she walked hastily towards the house. Stephanie met Mr Walker coming along a side path from the hill behind them.

'Magnificent, truly sensational, my dear young lady. I can't begin to thank you.'

'Don't thank me, thank Mrs Nayton. Here's Dare's parents coming to meet us.'

Greetings over, they moved into the house where Mrs Nayton showed some of the first sketches. Stephanie watched the pages and as they turned they seemed to be a constant reminder of their lives. Quick outlines of Alan, herself, their parents, other neighbours and farm scenes flashed before her eyes.

It seemed as though then she hadn't been alive, hadn't known the constant ache of loving Dare and the torment of the present situation, she thought sadly. When he walked in shortly before dinner, his eyes met hers challengingly. Stephanie hastily looked out of the window, but the blackness there gave her no comfort.

'If you want to see the garden, Stephanie, I'll escort you later.' The laughter was dangerously close in Dare's voice.

'If I want to stroll in the garden, I can do so in daylight, thank you,' said Stephanie softly.

'But in the moonlight there are certain flowers which hold more allure than in the heat of the day,' Dare continued.

Stephanie looked hopefully across the room where the other three were still studying the books. She took the drink Dare had poured for her. He studied her appearance. Without thinking she had worn an unusual bronze, gold and flame coloured silk dress.

'To a golden butterfly,' Dare toasted.

Stephanie looked into the amber contents of her glass. The light reflected from the angle of the crystal, sparkling brightly. To her relief Dare was called away at that moment and she could drink her sherry in a more relaxed way. The dinner was excellent. If it hadn't been for the fact that several times when she looked up she saw Dare watching her she could have enjoyed it, she thought— Dare and the director kept them entertained with stories of the art world and in spite of herself Stephanie was fascinated.

In such a cosmopolitan atmosphere Dare would be immediately at home she realised. She could only too well imagine the impression Dare would have created in the fashionable circles with his talent, good looks and rugged masculinity. After the meal they sat around on the comfortable chairs talking generally and Stephanie let her thoughts wander for a moment, then brought her attention back rapidly to listen more attentively.

'I agree with you, Stephanie is an interesting subject. However, I'm not interested in doing a portrait.'

Dare's voice had deepened, telling Stephanie his dislike of Mr Walker's suggestion clearly.

'It's just that having seen your talent for the portrait in those earlier sketches I think you should consider it as a possibility,' the director continued.

'Give it a try,' put in Dare's mother with a smile. 'Stephanie could sit for you at the weekends, I'm sure.'

Stephanie glanced pleadingly at Dare's father, who was quietly observing the scene.

'I rather think Stephanie has her own commitments,' he told the group.

Thankfully, Stephanie relaxed with a smile for her ally.

'Stephanie, if you take your car down the side of the old orchard you'll be able to drive right down to the studio. I'll meet you there and put the paintings in the car for you.'

Stephanie realised that Dare had quietly put an end to further discussion. She left Mr Walker still charming Dare's parents and slipped out to the car.

The outside lights enabled her to see and it took but a moment to drive round as Dare had suggested. The studio lights were on and she could see Dare tying a protective cover into place. She got out and unlocked the back door of the car. Dare carried out the first painting and leaned it carefully against the seat. Wordlessly he went back to collect the next one and positioned it with packing into place. He closed the door and Stephanie saw him throw an envelope on to the seat.

Surprised, she picked it up and looked at him.

'What is it?' she asked.

'Commission,' he said bluntly.

Stephanie handed it back to him unopened. 'That's not necessary.' She spoke quietly. 'It was your mother who suggested the trip.'

'You wouldn't have come otherwise?'

Stephanie didn't answer and she felt the tension leap between them. With an effort to break it down she gave an attempt at a chuckle.

'For one of your mother's meals, of course I would.'

The light from the studio highlighted the planes of Dare's face, leaving his eyes in shadow, so she could not read the expression there.

'The night plays tricks, Stephanie. This evening was very pleasant. Thank you for your company.'

She smiled at hearing the oddly formal phrases. 'I'm sure everybody enjoyed it, except when you were asked about painting me.'

'You were embarrassed?'

'Yes, of course. You've made your feelings very clear, Dare. For the sake of our families we have to appear to meet occasionally, but that doesn't mean we have to be together at other times.'

'Besides, it would limit your style with those men friends of yours.'

'That's not worthy of an answer.'

'Why? Are there too many to count?' Dare stood taut before her and his face looked hard. Stephanie was conscious of her breathing becoming ragged under the strain. She licked her lips and tried to look for a means to avoid the confrontation.

'Dozens!' she uttered weakly.

Dare stepped back abruptly. Stephanie almost ran to the driver's side and hurriedly started the motor, revving it in her anxiety to leave.

Mr Walker sat with a contented smile on his face and to Stephanie's relief was disinclined to talk, so the trip home was made in good time. Although Mat and Ray both urged her to have supper with them she shook her head, preferring to stay well away from her perceptive friends. Once on her own she drove rapidly back to her flat. Only as she lay sleepless in bed later did she wonder why Dare always seemed to upset her.

CHAPTER SIX

BECAUSE she had lain awake for so long the night before Stephanie stayed in bed luxuriating in a sleep-in on Saturday morning. She read for a while and hunger eventually drove her to get up. Once dressed she began tidying the flat and completed her washing and ironing. After cooking herself an early meal she drove off to the studio for the now familiar Saturday night shift.

For once she found it hard to inject warmth and lighthearted gaiety into the programme. As she played some of the pops she found her thoughts increasingly on Dare and Barbara, and she was glad once the programme reached Party Time, where the listeners' phone calls kept her on her mettle. The technician was the same one she had worked with the last few Saturday nights, and she was aware of his puzzled stare once or twice when her presentation was not as rapid as she would have liked.

'You OK, Stephanie?' he enquired.

'Just having an off day, or rather an off night,' confessed Stephanie.

'It happens now and then,' he said consolingly. 'I've got a fill timed to the news.'

Stephanie nodded gratefully. She would have forgotten the necessary instrumental record for the link with the commercial network. While the news was on she lined up the next two numbers and glanced through the commercials she had to announce. The cue lights blinked at her and she listened attentively picking up the station cue perfectly. She let the background swell a little before announcing the record, then slowly turned its volume, checking the sound level needle immediately beside the turntable. The last hour flew and she could tell the sheer effort of working had paid off.

'Want to come to a party, Stephanie?' asked the technician, as they closed the station.

'Not tonight, thanks. I think I should call it a long enough day.'

'There's a whole twenty-four hours ahead.'

For a moment Stephanie was tempted. 'Ask me another time, will you? I'd be poor company tonight.' She didn't add that she couldn't risk another encounter with Dare, and with her luck he would turn out to be at the same party.

By Sunday evening Stephanie was in a more positive frame of mind. She decided to have a long luxurious soak in a bubble bath and go to bed early. Deciding that she might as well go the whole way and select her prettiest nightwear, she took out a set which Mat had given her for her last birthday. It was a satiny fabric in a sheen of white tinged with hints of lemon and green. As it had more than a bridal hint about it, until this evening she had never worn it. Thinking that she was hardly likely to be a bride, she removed it from its tissue-lined box. It was far too pretty to remain in a drawer waiting for a dream to come true.

She savoured her bath, adjusting the hot tap with her toe now and then to keep the water warm. The bubbles had never been fluffier and they acted like an insulating layer. The level of water reached the stage where it was dangerous to move, and with a grin for her own sense of luxury she reluctantly climbed out, before the water cooled too much. Her hair she had protected in a cap, but it had still managed to get slightly damp and she quickly blow-dried it. Surveying herself in the mirror, she had to admit that the new night attire suited her. Her skin was all pink and pearly from the long soak and with her hair loose curling on to her shoulders there was a hint of spice in the slit side of the nightgown.

'You've read too many commercials, Stephanie Fernley!' she chuckled. She slipped on the matching wrap and went into the kitchen to make herself a cup of hot chocolate.

'Hardly champagne!' she toasted herself as she sat down on the big, comfortable old sofa. Her book was sitting on the arm and she picked it up. She had barely finished her drink when the peace was shattered by the doorbell.

'Dare!' she exclaimed.

'Your mother knew I was going to be in town today and she asked me to drop this in. Where do you want it?'

Stephanie looked at the large sack of potatoes with a hint of despair. Dare was smiling openly at her appearance as though she had worn it for his benefit.

'Have I called in at an inopportune time?' he asked with no hint of regret in his voice.

'Not in the slightest,' Stephanie answered, trying to keep cool. She felt intense chagrin that Dare should see her, but she did not want him to know that his presence could upset her so easily.

'Come in. I'll get the key to the garage. I'd like you to put the potatoes there.'

'Certainly, ma'am!'

As he put the sack down a moment later he murmured softly, 'You look especially tempting, Stephanie. Quite strikingly beautiful, in fact. Expecting company?'

'I was intending to go to bed early.' Stephanie spoke shortly. 'I was on duty last night.'

'So I heard. I wanted . . .'

Whatever he was about to say was cut short by the doorbell in the distance. Glancing up, Stephanie saw a well dressed young man armed with flowers and a folder. She was instantly aware of Dare's face becoming tight and hard. He gave her an annihilating glance, then turned and strode off to his car.

Stephanie slowly went up to the young man.

'Miss Fernley? Dad sent me in with these notes on leptospirosis. The breakthrough on the research into the disease on cattle is listed on page twenty-two. Mum sent in these flowers. She told me to tell you that she enjoys your programme.'

'Thank you very much.' Stephanie took the package from the lad's hands with a smile.

'Dad wasn't able to drop these notes earlier. The interview's tomorrow, isn't it?'

'That's right. I'm pleased to get them. I'm sure it will make riveting bedtime reading.'

The young man chuckled. 'Goodnight, Miss Fernley.'

'Goodnight; tell your mother the flowers are beautiful.'

Stephanie closed the door slowly. She reflected that the lad's timing could hardly have been more disastrous. After her convincing Dare that she was not expecting a caller, the arrival of a young man bearing flowers made her appear a liar. Recalling the look Dare had given her made her shudder.

The gladioli looked magnificent in a deep pottery vase, their colours picking up the bright tones of the painting. Sadly she wondered if tonight would have been another wasted opportunity to set the record straight with Dare. Gladioli were her mother's favourite flowers, and she wished her mother would have told her that she asked Dare to drop the potatoes in. If she had only known he was coming she could at least have been dressed in something slightly less seductive. If she had not antagonised Dare he would not have reacted so quickly when the young man arrived. If Dare had stayed he would have realised the young man was someone she had never met before.

If, if, if, if, thought Stephanie. A wry smile peeped out. If Dare only knew that instead of the scene he had envisaged she was sitting up with the notes of a cattle disease and a novel!

The telephone woke her the next morning and Stephanie focused on the clock in alarm. The hand pointing to seven reassured her.

'Good morning,' she answered sleepily.

'Stephanie, the baby's arrived—it's a girl!'

Stephanie shot upright in bed. 'Ray, that's great news. Congratulations! Tell me more.'

'Mat's fine, a bit tired, but we're both thrilled. She's so tiny, but she's all there. Do you know she's got fingernails that are so delicate you wouldn't believe it possible! Her hands are so small, but can she cling on to your finger. It's incredible! As strong as a lion.' Ray's voice was full of excitement.

'That's marvellous, Ray. Tell Mat I'll be thinking of her and I'll visit her tomorrow if that's convenient. I'm sure the baby's beautiful. It must be clever too, as it's picked such nice parents.'

'Thanks, Stephanie. I must ring a few more people, so I'd better go.'

Stephanie smiled as she replaced the receiver.

After she was dressed she dialled the florist. He usually did delightful arrangements for babies, including a series of little vases in the shape of bootees or prams, and Stephanie ordered one for Mat.

There was a trace of a chill in the air and as she walked along she noticed the chestnuts along the river Avon were turning brown. The summer had been so long she had begun to forget about the colder days of autumn. The river had little water and she crossed the bridge, stopping as usual to see any fish. Often she could pick out the trout or eels, but today the birds had the river to themselves. A few seagulls stood in a group on the bank, and a small red-billed one reminded her of the bird that she had seen at Birdlings Flat.

The early morning traffic sped past her and she turned for the studio, entering the building as Ray approached.

'I didn't expect to see you just yet,' she smiled. 'Would you and your uncle like to come for dinner this evening? You could have it before you go to see Mat if that's easier.'

'I will accept gladly. That's beaut, Stephanie. I'll bring Uncle along about six. Will that be too early?'

'No, that will be fine. Hospital visiting starts at seven and I know you'll want to be on time. You could leave your uncle with me and pick him up afterwards—that will give you the chance to be alone with Mat.'

She smiled at the look of relief on Ray's face. 'It won't be an elaborate meal, I'm afraid.'

'Don't worry! I wouldn't notice if I was eating straw or strawberries. The baby's got the most amazing blue eyes.'

Stephanie remembered another set of blue eyes as she went into her office. She put her research notes down and began checking her studio editing times. At least with work she could forget temporarily the owner of those blue eyes.

It was a busy day. Stephanie did the interview on leptospirosis, then followed up another couple of leads for other items. That evening's meal was a bright, happy occasion despite the rush, and after Ray had left Ted Walker and Stephanie continued discussing the art world. The high esteem in which the director held Dare's work was obvious and he told of several incidents which showed the extent of Dare's fame overseas. When he began to question her about butterflies, however, Stephanie felt uncomfortable. She was relieved when Ray arrived to pick up his uncle. At least the baby could oust Dare as a topic of conversation.

Her mail the next day contained two tickets for a show about to open in town. The accompanying letter confirmed the interview time Stephanie had already arranged. She was just checking her schedule when Ray walked in to thank her for the previous evening's meal.

'That's all right. You can do something for me,' she grinned. 'I need a record of the star's song as an introduction for an interview I'm doing tomorrow.'

'Wish I was meeting her. She's a fantastic singer,' breathed Ray.

'Well, I've two tickets for the show tomorrow night.

You find the record and you can use the other ticket.' She handed it over.

'Tremendous! I'll pick you up after I've seen Mat and the baby tomorrow night.'

At lunchtime Stephanie slipped out early to see Mat. Although it was not the usual time she was allowed to visit and admire the baby, and Mat was delighted. As Stephanie returned through the hospital corridors she wrinkled her nose at the distinctive hospital combination of polish, people and disinfectants. Vaguely she wondered on the possibilities of doing a documentary on the work involved in keeping such an establishment running, then grinned at herself. She was becoming as bad as Goldie—all work and no play. Again a smile played around her face. One person at least considered her the opposite!

Promptly at ten-thirty the next day Stephanie knocked on the door of the plushly decorated guest's suite, where the star of the show was staying. The job was a routine one for her, but as usual she had prepared thoroughly.

She was looking forward to meeting the star and was just wondering whether she would be as beautiful in real life as she seemed on the screen and in photos, when the door opened and she felt her smile freeze on her face at the sight of the dark-haired man.

'Good morning, Stephanie.'

Dare's voice was steady, but the cool hostility in his blue eyes was not disguised.

'Do come in.' He held the door open and gestured mockingly.

Stephanie recovered her wits as he introduced her to the star, who turned, holding out a welcoming hand.

'Neighbours, you said. Well, perhaps you're the reason

why this handsome male escaped all the girls overseas.' She smiled charmingly at Stephanie and indicated a chair. 'Dare is just a darling, isn't he?'

Beside her Dare smiled and Stephanie felt like throwing the recorder at him. She certainly didn't think him a darling. Abruptly she turned her attention to the recorder. She hoped she wouldn't have to do the interview with Dare standing right beside her. She couldn't even begin to think of the carefully timed phrases she had prepared earlier as an introduction. Her mind seemed to have gone completely blank.

'You don't mind my friend waiting while I do the interview, do you?' said the star. 'I've told him he'd have to wait a few minutes before he takes me off to see his etchings!'

The star chuckled at her own joke and Stephanie tried to force a smile. She caught Dare's eyes. He was daring her to ask the actress to throw him out. She forced her temper back, reminding herself that she was a professional, that the presence of one man listening should make no difference. She plugged in the microphone and hid her chagrin.

'Of course not.'

Sheer experience came to her rescue and she managed an introduction, then let the actress tell her own story. Possibly because of Dare she let the interview develop into a much longer one than she had intended.

Every part of her was aware when Dare walked quietly to the window, his gaze only for the busy scene below them. Equally she noted when he leaned against the wall, his stance that same lithe easy grace that had always attracted her. Distracted, she pulled herself back to the star's comments just in time to ask a final question. With relief she completed the closing remark and switched off the recorder.

The star smiled her thanks.

'I'm giving a small get-together after the show tonight. I do hope you and your escort will be able to come. Dare will tell you I usually get my own way,' she warned as she saw Stephanie's frown crease. 'Have you other plans?'

'No,' put in Stephanie wishing immediately that she had not told the truth for once.

'Good. I'll want to ask you what you thought of the show, so don't let me down.'

Stephanie flicked a glance at Dare. He was positively enjoying her discomfiture, she realised. He was waiting for her to turn down the invitation. Inwardly she gritted her teeth. As calmly as she could she stood up.

'My friend and I will be delighted to accept. Thank you for your time.'

Feeling pleased with her own acting ability, she moved towards the door, but Dare automatically took the recorder from her fingers.

'I'll carry that as far as the lift.'

He opened the door for her and ushered her out with such an obvious charm Stephanie felt her temper rise again.

The lift was almost opposite the door and she pressed the button, hoping it would come at once. To her relief it opened immediately.

'Bringing your young Romeo tonight?' Dare asked as he placed the recorder in beside her. He straightened and looked her in the eyes. He added his final shot, firing it as he released the door. 'Still, at least he wouldn't be married!'

The door swished shut and Stephanie felt it descend instantaneously, cutting off her indignant protest. Boiling with anger, she marched back to the studio. She wasn't helped when she replayed the tape and heard her infantile questions. Only the charm of the star and her own experience had saved the tape. Ruthlessly she began editing it into shape and just finished in time to go on air.

Dressing for the show that evening, Stephanie found herself still angry with Dare. She was glad of Ray's escort; at least Dare wouldn't know him nor the fact that he was married. They were likely to see each other, but only from a distance, and she would have to control her feelings as the theatre was hardly the place to have a showdown. At least not in the dress circle, she thought. She added a dab of her favourite perfume for luck just as Ray pulled up to collect her. They could leave the car in Ray's usual park just around the corner from the magnificent Town Hall, and they chatted amiably as they entered the foyer.

Stephanie's eyes picked out the distinguished tall, dark-haired figure by the staircase attire and she found her temper raising again. He glanced across at her, and his eyes challenged hers. Deliberately she looked away as icily as she could. Feeling at least as if she had won a major victory, Stephanie floated upstairs and along to their seats in the dress circle. All but two seats next to hers were occupied in their row, and as the lights dipped warningly she stared in disbelief as a familiar man accompanying a pretty blonde entered the row.

He sat down completely relaxed, Stephanie thought, as she gazed rigidly ahead. Her whole body was seething with a mixture of anger, frustration and despair, and when he placed his arm along her seat rest she tightened her knuckles to hide her annoyance. The first act passed with everyone else enjoying it thoroughly, conceded Stephanie. All she was aware of was the magnetism of the man beside her and the alarm which rippled through her each time he moved a muscle.

To her intense relief Barbara and Dare left their seats at half-time after a perfunctory introduction.

'Ray, would you mind swopping seats?' Stephanie asked.

'Can't you see? Here, you should have told me earlier.'

Ray moved over obligingly, and Stephanie resettled herself and began to feel better immediately. Dare would not know that she had deliberately changed seats to avoid him, but he would have a shrewd idea. At least with Ray acting as a buffer Dare would be unlikely to pass any comment likely to lead to a scene.

'I'm enjoying it immensely,' Ray commented. 'Here, I don't think you've even glanced at the programme.'

'Thanks. I read it before I interviewed the star yesterday.' She saw Dare head along the row and took the offered programme. 'Just one item I wanted to check.'

She knew she was hiding, but she didn't care. Until the play started again she didn't want to get involved in discussion with Dare and Ray. She knew what Dare would think if he found out Ray was married.

The second half Stephanie managed to enjoy, and when the final curtain rang down she joined in the enthusiastic applause. While she was waiting in the aisle it was natural that Ray and Barbara exchanged views, and Stephanie was aware of Dare's silence and her own stillness.

'A different Romeo tonight,' he commented quietly. 'Seems a nice guy.'

'Ray's in the programme section at work. He helped me with the interview material,' she explained. 'He's an old friend.'

'You've more lovers than a tree has leaves!' He bit the words off, and Stephanie felt her anger rise. She was about to snap an answer when Ray took her arm.

'This way, Stephanie,' he said gaily. 'What a nice girl Barbara is. I've told her to come and visit us some time. Can't say I've impressed your other friend, he keeps looking at me as though I was something the cat dragged in. Sure he's not a trifle possessive over you?'

'Dare? Heavens, no! We're barely on speaking terms. We were about to break into one of our usual rows when you nudged us forward just then.'

'Sounds difficult,' Ray laughed, and Stephanie chuckled too.

'He's a real ice mountain. I think I'd better watch for avalanches.' He grinned unashamedly.

They were greeted at that moment by one of the cast and welcomed to the party. A few minutes later Merle Hilton, the star, entered and soon drinks were circulating. Stephanie watched as Dare introduced Barbara and she took care to keep well out of the way until Dare was welcomed by another group.

'Miss Fernley, you were most efficient this morning. I heard the interview while I was in Dare's car. My agent will be pleased.'

'Thanks to you. This is a colleague, Ray Jenkins.'

'Splendid. I hope you enjoyed the show, Mr Jenkins.'

'Immensely. My wife's going to be very jealous when I tell her I met you.'

'Ray's wife has just presented him with a baby,' explained Stephanie.

'Then we must toast the new little one. Is it a boy or a girl?'

A few minutes later the champagne was being poured and Ray's proud status proclaimed. The atmosphere was entirely convivial except for the pair of blue eyes which seemed to be following her, thought Stephanie. She knew just what Dare was thinking, and it was unfortunate she had babbled about the baby to the star.

Ray became slightly mellow with all the attention and the extra drinks poured for him, and Stephanie guessed then that he had not stopped for a meal.

'Old ice man of the mountains is looking at me,' said Ray a little later. 'Do you know, Stephanie, I think he's a bit jealous. Let's give him something to think about.'

With impish glee he pulled her into a dance, propelling her rapidly to a dark corner where their figures could scarcely be seen.

'Ray!' protested Stephanie.

'Ssshh! Let me tell you a story about the night I asked Mat to marry me. I'd been trying to think of the best way to ask her, and then this other chap came up and asked her for a dance. He whipped her off into a shady spot and I went through agonies. I suddenly woke up to what a chump I was, so I tapped him on the shoulder and told Mat she was going to marry me. Mat said she would, so long as I would stop trying to do a waltz to a tango.'

'Sounds like Mat,' smiled Stephanie.

'So a little spot of jealousy can help the cause of true romance,' ended Ray with a grin. 'Besides, you can tell he's not in love with the blonde and beautiful Barbara.'

Stephanie glanced over at Dare. The glare on his face was a trick of the lighting, she told herself. Remembering that Dare was not in love with her, she knew that Ray's idea would just serve to convince Dare that she was flirting with another married man.

Ray moved unsteadily so she was supporting him momentarily.

'Ray, you're a lovely man, but your plan won't work, because there's no love lost between Dare and me. Look, it's the new day already, and both of us have a lot to do. Really, I'd like to go home.'

'Is that the time?' queried Ray disbelievingly. 'It's been fun, I only wish Mat could have come with us. Let's say our farewells and get going.'

Hastily Stephanie checked that Dare was talking to friends before thanking their hostess. She didn't particularly want to face his hostile blue eyes again. A few minutes later they arrived at Ray's car.

'Let me drive, Ray,' she said. 'I think it would be better.'

'Fine—I'm sleepy. Think I had too much champagne.'

Relieved, Stephanie drove the car round to Ray's house.

'You take the car and pick me up in the morning on your way to work,' he told her.

Stephanie watched as he negotiated the path to his front door as though he was walking on eggs, then she turned the car back to her flat. She locked it carefully, wishing she could park it beside her own in the garage. It would have to stay out on the street all night, and she wondered if Dare would see it. If he did he would probably have an even lower opinion of her than before.

She decided that the chance of Dare seeing the car was remote. She settled into bed and pulled the pillow into a comfortable shape, her mind going over Ray's words. Could there be any truth in them, by any chance? Was there a grain of truth?

'Stop indulging in fantasies,' she admonished herself sleepily. All the same, she went to sleep with a smile on her face.

'Stephanie, you're a pal!' Ray's greeting showed only a trace of sheepishness.

'What time are you picking up Mat and the baby?' asked Stephanie to divert his attention, as she slid over to let Ray take the driver's seat. By the time they reached the station both of them were thinking of the day ahead. Stephanie went into her office thinking of the documentary she was compiling on accidents on the road and she had three interviews arranged for the day. She knew she would be tired before the day was over.

At four-thirty she pushed her seat back and threw the last tape into her drawer. She longed for some fresh air. Gathering her handbag, she deftly applied some make-up, then decided to walk through to the square and catch a bus to the beach. It took only a few moments to put the thought into action and she was almost surprised how quickly she reached her destination. With a rueful smile for her high heels and stockings she slipped into the changing shed and removed them, along with her jacket. A minute later she ran along the sandy shore, revelling in the space and the tangy sea air. The beach was nearly deserted and she guessed that the younger families had already left and the older ones were still at work. She could see one or two people further down and a man was sheltered by a sunbleached tree trunk abandoned by the waves.

Leaving her pile of shoes, stockings and jacket on the dry sand, she ran childlike to the water. The water tipped her toes with the sea foam and she ran back and forth, delighting in the waves, gradually allowing the water to creep over her toes then her feet, then her ankles. A larger wave unexpectedly surged and she ran back, laughter on her lips. Hastily hitching up her skirt, she wished she had taken her swimming togs. The water was still warm from the long summer. Her hair was too restricted for such a place and she pulled out the clips, then thrust her fingers through it to free it. Satisfied, she gave herself up to the fun of her game, running out to meet the waves and jumping when they crested. The simple amusement delighted her, challenging her to risk further splashes on her skirt. She was watching now for the bigger waves which could so easily drench her, and seeing one coming she moved hastily backwards to avoid it. Pain stabbed her foot and she let out a short instinctive cry. She hobbled back, storklike, supporting her foot where the blood was running.

'Steady, Stephanie!'

Surprise almost made her overbalance, but Dare's firm hand supported her.

'Hold on to me for a moment. I think it's more of a surface wound from the look of it.'

'What are you doing here, Dare?' she demanded.

'Same as you, seeing the sea,' he answered teasingly.

His blue eyes glinted, like the sunlight breaking through a wave, thought Stephanie irrationally.

'Put your foot in the water and the salt will help clean it.

Then I'll tie it up.' He supported her to the sand and deftly tied a large white handkerchief in place. 'That will keep the worst of the sand out till you can get a bandage on it. I'll just remove that object if I can locate it and get rid of it.'

He strode back into the sea and a minute later she saw him stoop and pick up an old can. With a powerful throw he pitched it with complete accuracy across the beach and into a rubbish tin.

Despite herself Stephanie found her smile matched his.

'Had your tetanus shot?' he asked. She nodded. She found herself oddly bemused by his near-nakedness, his sheer size and virility. His hair was still curling slightly around his face, and on the back of his neck, and she guessed that he must have been swimming only moments before. She felt a sudden urge to sweep the curls back with her fingers, then remembered his antagonism of the night before. She stood up with an effort.

'I'll return your handkerchief later, thank you,' she said stiffly.

Dare ignored the remark. 'I'll help you to your car. Where have you parked it? I doubt if you'd be able to drive on that foot.'

'Don't worry,' put in Stephanie. She knew she couldn't take much more of Dare being kind. 'I came by bus, so there's no need to concern yourself.'

'My car's just over the other side. I'll leave you up by the sea wall on the seat while I drive it up. There's no point in being silly.'

Stephanie had the distinct impression that he would pick her up and carry her if she looked likely to move, and she subsided into the seat. Her foot was throbbing and she loosened the tight bandage for a moment, then re-tightened it when Dare drove up.

'I'm sorry to be a nuisance, but my clothes are still on the beach.' she told him.

'You seem to be overdressed rather than under,' quipped Dare, his eyes twinkling. 'Relax. I picked up shoes, panty-hose, jacket and handbag. Was that all?'

Hastily Stephanie pulled down her damp skirt and slid on to the seat. Dare's sketching blocks and his clothes lay on the back seat. He reached past her and grabbed a shirt, pulling it on with scant respect for buttons. The lean powerful muscularity of his legs took her eye and she hastily glanced away. A faint chuckle told her he had seen her reaction.

'I can't help my beautiful body,' he murmured wickedly, eyes dancing.

'If you're insisting on driving me home, please drive,' snapped Stephanie irately.

'Certainly, ma'am.' Again the gleam, and a deferential touch to his forelock, reminded her of earlier days. Stephanie looked out of her window so she would not have to hide the chagrin she felt.

'Did I tie that too tight? I'll pull over and readjust it.'

'It's fine, thank you.' She didn't went to prolong the journey by even a few moments. She was relieved when they pulled up outside the flat.

'You look a bit pale, but otherwise OK,' said Dare as he turned her face around. He walked quickly round to open the car door for her and Stephanie hoped he could not hear the thumping of her heart as he helped her across to the flat. Why should her face tingle where his fingers touched? Surely she couldn't still be in love with him?

CHAPTER SEVEN

DARE took the key and she saw him recognise her key ring. He had given it to her on her eighteenth birthday, she remembered.

'That was a long time ago, Stephanie.'

She met his eyes steadily, then found his hand supporting her to the couch.

'I'll fix it,' she said quietly.

'Much easier for me,' said Dare, and went into the bathroom and pulled out the first aid kit she kept there. A moment later he washed the wound, carefully removing the tiny grains of sand. The silence between them grew as he steadily applied salve, then bandaged it.

'Beautiful things, feet,' admired Dare at last, as he placed her leg carefully beside the other one. 'Lovely bones—a wonderful piece of engineering.'

Unnerved, Stephanie fiddled with the box. Dare took it from her and replaced it in the bathroom.

'Rest tonight, Stephanie,' he ordered.

'I had intended to. I was out late last night.'

Too late she saw the flash of ice return to his face.

'I wasn't going to mention it, Stephanie, but perhaps it's as well to bring it out to the open. Quite frankly, your relationships with the opposite sex appal me. That chap last night—was it true his wife was in the home with a new baby?'

'Yes, she is. They're both old, dear friends.'

'Some friend you are! His car, or I presume it was his, outside your flat all night!'

'It was his car. I drove it home,' she told him.

'And do you want me to believe that after the performance the two of you put on at the party, you sat and played tiddleywinks all night?'

'No, I went to bed. I dropped Ray off at his flat, as he wasn't fit to drive, that's all.'

She looked up at Dare and caught a glimpse of his face. Strangely enough, she thought he looked as if he wanted to believe her.

'You always seem to catch me in the wrong, like the night you called in with the potatoes,' she protested.

'Romeo waiting while you did your innocent maiden routine?' Dare almost shot the words at her.

'I didn't know he was coming—honestly. He was simply dropping off some papers for his father, who happens to be an expert on leptospirosis.'

'And the flowers? Were they from his maiden aunt?'

'No. His mother, if you must know.'

She bent her head dejectedly. She felt dispirited, knowing how fanciful her story sounded.

'Stephanie, there's no need to lie to me.'

Dare said it quietly, but his eyes were almost black with anger. He strode out of the door and a moment later the roar of the car sounded like a snarl of rage. Stephanie lay back on the couch, emotionally exhausted, her feelings throbbing in time to the pain in her foot.

All through the night the pain kept her awake and she slept at last only briefly before dawn. There was no joy in working that day, and she was glad she could relax fo once as she was playing tapes she had made earlier, including the one on the cattle disease.

As it played, she could see again Dare's face as he accused her and the cue lights had to blip several times before she snapped back to the programme. Her professional training helped as she made the back announcement, adding that the speaker's wife had some of the best gladioli she had seen and that she was still enjoying them in her flat.

She announced the next interview with a concentration that forced out all thought, other than the job in hand. It was a relief to get out of the studio at lunchtime and, invited to join some of her colleagues, she readily agreed. At least their conversation kept her mind occupied.

The rest of the week sped by. Her foot healed and soon she knew there would only be a faint red mark as a reminder. She wished her feelings could heal as quickly.

At the weekend she thought twice about going home. There would be open warfare between Dare and herself after their last confrontation. Any future meetings would be fraught with difficulties. Yet if she stayed away when she was not on duty it would create problems. Dare would no doubt think she had stayed away because of him, and although it would be true, Stephanie didn't want him to know it.

Work decided the issue as she had an interview to be done late on Friday. She decided to go out to the farm after she'd tidied the flat on Saturday. Ray and Mat invited her round to have dinner on Friday night and she went, armed with another toy for the baby. She had already brought several dainty clothes for the new arrival and had given them to Mat earlier. The evening was a great success and the new baby behaved as a model, just as Ray had promised.

Mat, wearing a dark blue dress, looked like a medieval Madonna as she fed the baby, and Stephanie wondered wistfully if she would ever have a child of her own.

As she drove back to the flat she knew she would miss her friends when they shifted to Timaru. Ray's appointment had been announced in the last circular. At least, she reminded herself, she could drive down and see them frequently.

Thinking about the young couple Stephanie decided that she should organise a farewell party for them. Numbers would have to be limited because of the size of the flat, and that would be the biggest problem, as the staff all knew and liked Mat and Ray. Supper she could arrange herself with a little help from one or two others and her mother would be sure to do some baking.

Saturday morning flew as Stephanie cleaned the flat and then flung some gear into the car and set off for the farm. The sun-scorched, golden paddocks glared in the heat and Stephanie remembered the interview she had done earlier with one of the fire chiefs. The long summer had turned into a drought and the evidence was seen with the lack of stock. The farmers would be glad when the autumn rains fell. Even the trees looked burnt, she noted as she pulled into the familiar drive. Her mother was in her garden and she looked up as Stephanie rolled her car to a stop.

'Hullo, darling. Was it hot in town?'

'Not too bad, Mum. Your garden still surviving?'

'Only just. I'm glad I put that extra mulch on. It helped.'

'You sound like a commercial!' teased Stephanie, her eyes twinkling as she bent to give her mother a hug.

'Probably where I came in!'

'How's Mat and the baby? You were going to have a meal with them last night, I think you said.'

'That's right. They're fine. The baby's beautiful.'

'Well, of course. I remember when you were born and Alan and Dare thought you were the most delightful treasure. Whenever Dare came you'd cling on to his finger, and with Alan you'd always pull his hair. Poor Alan! I solved the problem by cutting his hair a different way. So then you started reaching for Dare's. I swear you did it to tease. My goodness, how time flies! Why don't you invite Mat and Ray out for the day one weekend soon? I'd love to see the baby.'

'It will have to be soon, Mum, Ray's been promoted to Timaru.'

'Timaru? You'll miss them, dear. Still, it's not too far away.'

'Yes. They're thrilled, as it's their home town.'

'How lovely for their families. I do envy some people.'

Stephanie knew what her mother was thinking even if she was too tactful to express the thought. Her mother had hinted before that it was time Alan found the right girl and got married, and for herself Stephanie knew that her mother felt that the sooner Prince Charming came along the better. But, reflected Stephanie, in her own fairy tale Prince Charming had become the angry king who didn't even like the princess. Did he?

Stephanie picked a cluster of deep blue black grapes. They were delicious.

'Pick some, Stephanie, then you can run a boxful up to Naytons'. I gave the first few bunches to them the other day, their vine is later than ours,' commented Mrs Fernley.

'Fine, Mum. I was thinking of asking you to do some baking, I want to give Mat and Ray a party before they leave.'

'A party? What do you want? Savouries? Pavlovas? Pizzas?'

'You've got your sleeves rolled up already, Mum!' Stephanie smiled. 'Actually we won't need too much as I know some of the other girls will help. The numbers will have to kept down as I haven't the room in the flat.'

'The flat? Darling, you might be able to swing a cat in your lounge, but not much more. You can't hold it there. I've a much better idea. We can hold it here. I can just see it now. We can have the pool and put up the outdoor lights and your father and Alan and Dare can organise the barbecue. We can have dancing on the verandah and in the lounge and have the dining room free for supper afterwards. Oh, it will be lovely fun!'

Stephanie felt the ground open in front of her. The last thing she wanted was to be forced into a situation where she would have to see Dare and Barbara. Yet in the face of her mother's enthusiasm she felt sick. Her mother would enjoy the occasion tremendously and it was true that their home was ideal for entertaining.

'Stephanie, you've quite cheered me up. I was feeling so down with this heat, you're better than a shower of rain.'

'Some compliment!' laughed Stephanie. She knew she had lost. 'It would be lovely to hold the party here. Would three weeks away be too short notice? I know next week Ray and Mat are going to Timaru for the weekend to have a look at flats and houses. They're hoping to buy one of their own this time. They leave in four weeks.'

'Talk it over with them, but two or three weeks should be all right here. I'd better give your father fair warning, and see if it's all right with him. I don't think we've got anything planned.'

Stephanie picked another bunch and turned for her bedroom. She changed into her old shorts and a top. Sauntering outside again, she saw her father's horse shake his head at her over the fence. She picked out a carrot as she went by the vegetable bed and handed it over to the chestnut, who whinnied with delight.

'I haven't ridden you for ages,' she told the horse. 'Not since Dare returned.'

On impulse she ran back to the shed and collected a bridle and saddle. Within a few moments she had fastened the straps and having checked them, she put her foot into the stirrup and swung on to the broad back. Two minutes later she went cantering down towards the back of the farm. Close to she could see the effects of the drought and the stubble left in the wheat paddock where the crop had been harvested reminded her that her father had been pleased with the quality, if not the quantity. The bakers would be pleased with the long dry season. The bush which joined the Nayton and Fernley properties came into view and Stephanie turned away. She didn't want to face the totara tree and its memories.

Cantering quietly off in a different direction, as she wanted to avoid the short cut past Dare's studio, she was startled when a shot rang out. The giant horse leapt into

action, turning straight for the safety of his home paddock.
Stephanie found herself unable to control the horse as he
raced past the long flat. Deciding that it was possibly best
to let him run before attempting to calm him, she concentrated merely on staying on. Her plan was beginning to
work when a second shot rang out and the horse panicked.
Throwing his front legs back, he reared, and Stephanie
fell, crashing heavily on to the ground. The thrumming of
the horse's hooves sounded a mad tattoo as the chestnut
tore away. Gingerly, Stephanie rolled over on the ground.
She was considerably shaken by her fall but knew she had
been lucky. Her lips curled into a grin at her own unexpected predicament. The chestnut had the sweetest manners and was such a quiet horse that she had completely
forgotten that he was terrified of loud noises, such as
gunshots or fire crackers. She felt indignant that someone
could have been using a gun, then she remembered
shamefacedly that her own ride had been on impulse. If
she had asked her mother she would have been told to
wait.

Three more shots rang out in quick succession and she
stood up, identifying the sound as coming from the bush.
She thanked her lucky stars that she had not entered the
bush on her ride. The sound of running feet made her
turn.

'Dare! What's the matter?' she demanded.

'Thank God you're OK! Your mother rang me to stop
you. She was sure you'd take the long path past the studio.
I went up to the ridge and saw you riding like some
long-forgotten Valkyrie and then the horse turned down
here. Next thing no rider. I'm not up to running the sub
four-minute mile, but I must have come close!'

'Thank you for checking I'm all right, though.' Stephanie knew her thanks were ragged. 'A little injured pride, perhaps.'

He smiled, a deep slow smile that sent her pulses surging.

'You appear to be in one piece. You've grazed your arm and your leg, but otherwise there doesn't appear to be any damage. Come on and I'll take you back to the studio and clean you up.'

'I'm fine—I'd better go home, Mum will probably be worried.'

'That's why I suggested my place. It will take you twenty minutes to walk home.'

'I can be there in five minutes taking the cut between the bush.'

'Are you quite sure you didn't land on that stubborn head of yours?'

Stephanie remembered the firing in the bush and nodded. 'I suppose I'd better.'

'Ever gracious, my lady.'

She bit her lip with chagrin and flicked her hair back from around her face. The last person she wanted to see her in old shorts and brief top was Dare. It seemed as if she would have to walk with him across the fields and then have to allow him to patch her up again. Her leg and hip ached and her elbow felt sore, but under Dare's glance she straightened herself, determined that he should not know that his presence upset her far more than a toss from a horse.

'Allow me.' Dare held out his hand as they approached the fence and Stephanie took it, feeling oddly pleased. Dare's hand felt warm and comforting. Pain rocked through her as she climbed and she was glad of Dare's support after he had helped her over. She was surprised how reluctant she was to let his hand go. She shoved her hand into her pocket, annoyed with herself for her action, but not daring to further the tiny moment of peace between them.

A surreptitious peep from under her eyelids showed a hint of a curve to Dare's lips, as though he had been very much aware of her reasons for restricting her hand once the fence was past. At the next fence the problem did not arise, as he had led their way at an angle so that they were able to go through the gate.

'That better?' he enquired with an infuriating smile. 'Never mind, not far to go now.'

Stephanie nodded, not trusting herself to speak. She felt that whatever she said would be wrong.

'I didn't think you would be home this weekend,' he commented politely, as the silence between them lengthened.

'I didn't have to work,' she said shortly.

'You know, Stephanie, you continually surprise me. For such a butterfly, you do appear to work quite hard. I heard your programme the other morning. It appears I owe you an apology.'

She looked at him disbelievingly, her eyebrows forming a puzzled frown.

'Leptospirosis and young Romeo,' explained Dare. 'You had an interview on the subject. I'm sorry, Stephanie—I believe I accused you unjustly.'

Stephanie searched his face, but there was only the expression of regret. She wondered if the fall off the horse might have been providential. It had at least allowed her to spend time with Dare and he was in a mood to listen to explanations.

Hesitating, she wondered how she could explain the sequence which had led to their break.

'Dare, I've been wanting to explain,' she began.

'You don't have to, Stephanie. You told me the truth and I found it easier to believe otherwise.'

They had arrived at the studio and Stephanie could see that Dare had been busy painting as he had abandoned the brush and the door was wide open. A large canvas was facing her and Dare moved rapidly to turn it away.

'Come upstairs and ring your mother. I'll make some coffee.'

Stephanie would have liked to have returned to the subject of explanations, but she knew her mother would be in a panic. Perhaps, she thought, she could tell Dare over coffee. She moved towards the staircase and the angle of the stairs made her gasp with pain. The sound brought Dare to her side.

'Hold on to me,' he commanded.

For a moment she allowed herself the luxury of resting against him, feeling the warmth of his sympathy. The hardness of his body and the protective gesture of his arms around her made her throat ache.

'Hold it! You must have given yourself more of a bump than you realised. There's no need for you to go upstairs, I'll bring you down a drink.'

The pain waves had subsided and she shook her head. 'I'm fine.'

Dare ignored her comment and led her over to a long couch at one end of the studio. 'I only had it fitted last week, just in time for your act,' he told her.

His grin lit the gleams in his blue eyes, as Stephanie indignantly rose to the bait. Seeing his expression, she subsided.

'I'll ring your mother and put her fears at rest.'

Dare left her, taking the stairs two at a time with effortless ease. Stephanie propped another cushion behind herself and tried to see if there were any signs of a bruise. She was glad to have a moment to compose herself. The last teasing comment had reminded her of happier times with Dare.

A sketchbook lay almost hidden under the couch where the artist must have dropped it. Stephanie stared at the sketch of a foot which was all she could see on the page, then she reached for it. The book slid out open at a page covered in sketches of a foot. Despite herself, she felt a smile tickle her mouth. She was sure the sketches were based on her own feet. A hasty comparison soon satisfied her. A sketch of her big toe still with a faint scar on its side where she had cut it years ago proved it. Surprised that Dare still remembered it and noted it in the sketch, she was poring over the page when she heard him return down the stairs.

'Mine, I believe.' He removed the book from her suddenly nerveless fingers. Closing it, he put it out of reach. Stephanie felt uncomfortable. Quite obviously the old times when she had been allowed to look at his drawings had disappeared. He gave her the mug of coffee and the friendly camaraderie of a few moments before had gone. This was a stern unsmiling stranger, tall, aloof and totally unapproachable. Stephanie's heart sank. Dare's attitude could not have shown his disapproval more clearly. The coffee tasted bitter in her mouth and she put down the mug.

'Thank you, I'll go home now.' Stephanie struggled to sit up, but her leg muscles cramped, causing her to pull her face muscles in a grimace.

'I think you'd be better resting for a few moments. I'll go and get my car.'

Dare's words were clipped and unsympathetic. Quite obviously he thought her last wince had been a deliberate cry for sympathy. He finished his drink and took his keys from their holder by the door. A moment later he was gone.

Stephanie wanted to flee from the room, but her stiffened muscles made it difficult. Awkwardly she pulled herself upright and found that once she was standing the pain lessened. By the time she reached the door she guessed she could manage the walk home. By the time Dare returned with the car she could be halfway across the paddock, and she decided that would show him she did not need his help. The worst was going down the steps, but she gritted her teeth and managed to make it past the fence before Dare drove up beside her.

'Don't be entirely ridiculous!' he snapped.

Despite his words his touch was gentle as he helped her into the car. His hands, long and sensitive, had surprising strength and his touch seemed to burn through her skin. He drove the car slowly so that the bumps of the paddock were minimal and she knew that if she had waited and let him pick her up at the sudio as he had suggested there would have been none.

'There you are, Miss Stubborn,' Dare said softly, as hey pulled up a few moments later in front of the familiar armhouse.

'Why do we fight, Dare?' asked Stephanie almost to herself.

A smile softened the harsh rugged lines of his face as he helped her out again.

'Can't you, with your knowledge of men, work that out, Staphanie?'

Puzzled, she searched his face for a further clue.

'What do you mean?'

The blue eyes met hers and she found herself taking an instinctive step backwards, her mouth dry.

'I'm just a man, Stephanie.' Dare's voice was barely a whisper above her ear, and Stephanie felt her heart race as he ran his finger along the shoulder line of her top. She had never been so aware of his sexuality and so conscious of his attraction for her.

'Stephanie, bring Dare in for a cuppa, dear.' Mrs Fernley's voice shattered the moment as effectively as crystal on concrete.

'Give your mother my regrets, I've a painting that I don't want to leave.'

Dare gave her a slight push in the direction of the house and strode back to his car. The motor revved once and then he was gone.

Slowly Stephanie made her way along the hall, her blood ceasing its pounding gradually. She forced herself to breathe deeply several times, knowing it was a quick way to regain control. She felt as if the hot pools of Rotorua had suddenly yawned at her feet.

'Stephanie, you look very pale. Are you sure you didn't hurt yourself? Perhaps there's something broken?' her mother asked anxiously.

'It feels like it, Mum.' She added silently to herself, 'Bu

once before I got over a broken heart and I will again.'
Aloud she finished, 'I'll probably look like an advertise-
ment for a paint shop tomorrow, a rainbow of colours!'

'I knew Dare would stop you. For a moment I panicked—I'd forgotten about you riding the horse.'

'I should have mentioned it. I'd better go out and see
he's all right.'

'I've taken the gear from him and turned him loose in
the paddock. He's shaken, but all right.'

'Thanks, Mum.' Stephanie leaned forward and hugged
her mother. 'I'll get on with tea, shall I?'

'No, dear, I've organised it already. You rest for a
while.'

Stephanie went to her room gladly. There she could rub
her tender spots and remember the events of the morning.
Dare running to see she was all right; the look on his face;
the tenderness as he helped her over the fence and his
apology as they walked together back to the studio. Their
amity had not lasted long, within minutes she had found
the sketchbook and Dare's blistering anger had dismayed
her. As she had sat beside him in the car the tenseness and
awareness of each other had been tangible. When she had
asked him wistfully why they always fought he had given
her a double-edged answer. Desire was far from love,
Stephanie reminded herself.

Back at work the next week she found her bruises turning
the promised rainbow of colours. Being ribbed about her
toss on the air made it very public, and one of the listeners
to ring and commiserate was a well-known jockey.
Stephanie seized the opportunity to do a lighthearted
Times I wished I could forget' topic for a series. The

events well known people found embarrassing but could later laugh at proved popular, although not all were suitable for broadcasting.

Goldie, listening to Friday's programme as a matter of routine, sent his congratulations. Stephanie had just erased the successful tape when Ray popped into her office.

'Stephanie—we're going down to Timaru the next two weekends; we've already lined up some possible houses to look at, so the party would be fine the following weekend. Mat's really excited about it. Are you sure the mob won't be too much for your parents? It sounds great.'

'Mum's looking forward to it. I'll give her a ring and confirm it. Give me a list of your other friends and I'll see they get an invitation and a map.'

'We don't want them ending up at the wrong place.'

'Mrs Nayton wouldn't mind. They'll be going to the party too. Dare and his father will be helping with the barbecue.'

'Dare? Isn't that your painter friend? I'm looking forward to seeing him again. Come to think of it, Mat mentioned that she'd like to meet him too.'

'She'll have her chance at the party,' promised Stephanie, with a cheerfulness she was far from feeling.

The burr of the desk telephone interrupted them and Ray waved, before disappearing, leaving Stephanie to answer the call.

'Good afternoon, Stephanie Fernley speaking.'

'Hullo, dear, are you coming home this weekend?'

Stephanie thought of Dare and knew that she needed more time before she faced him again. If the cure was to proceed she would have to avoid him as much as possible.

'Sorry, Mum. A group of us are going out on Saturday night and there's also a possibility of an interview with a character I've been trying to reach for ages. I'll be home the next weekend, though.'

Mentally she added that Dare was due to be away on a painting trip which Alan had mentioned.

'I might even take a couple of days off and pre-record the programmes as I've got a pile of leave stacking up. Then we could organise the party food together.'

'That would be lovely—I've already made some pizzas and savouries. I'll get Alan to drop one in for you. I'll get him to parcel up some grapes. We've got a super crop this year.'

'Which reminds me, did Aunt Olivia get some? I forgot about it after my fall.'

'Of course, dear. I saw Dare and gave them to him. I gave him a big box to take in to Barbara too. What a charming girl she is! So attractive and so modest. She's very artistic. She was out here the other day and she gave me a beautiful plate with enamel that she'd fired. It's lovely. I really wish Alan could find a girl like Barbara. The two of them get on so well together. As a matter of fact . . .' Mrs Fernley suddenly stopped. 'Darling, you mustn't let me run on when you are at work. I must let you get busy. Byebye.'

Stephanie put down the phone slowly. She felt sick inside. It sounded as though Dare and Barbara were very close. Perhaps her mother was in the possession of a secret. Were the two of them shortly to announce their engagement? Was that why Dare had built his studio and living accommodation the minute he arrived home?

Stephanie knew a sharp agony. It didn't seem possible

that Dare could be going to marry. If he was in love with Barbara, why would he have reacted so strongly when he had thought she, Stephanie, was having an affair with a married man? Somewhere, something didn't add up. Wryly she admitted to herself that it was probably because Dare had regarded her as a friend for so long that he felt able to comment. Stephanie shook her head, instinct told her the powerful chemistry between Dare and herself had nothing to do with the fact he had known her from the day she was born.

She picked up a pencil and began doodling lightly on the back of the tape box. The trouble was simply that Dare had such a sensual, virile appeal, she told herself. His tall strong muscular body was a part of it, but only a part; there was an extra quality about him which others could appreciate. He could be charming, witty or downright stubborn and thoroughly obnoxious, Stephanie told herself. Most of the time where she was concerned, it was the latter.

Sighing, she looked at the box, and immediately pulled her thoughts together. The completely recognisable sketch with the icy chips for eyes stared back at her with more than a hint of arrogance. Hastily she took a rubber and erased the marks, wishing she could erase the image from her mind just as easily. The office junior came in just as she was putting the box in the tray on her desk.

'Stephanie, this letter seems to have been put in the wrong pile this morning. I'm sorry, I don't quite know how it happened. It's an inter-office one.'

'It happens!' Stephanie said reassuringly to the conscience-stricken junior. 'Thanks for telling me.'

As the junior went Stephanie glanced at the envelope

and smiled as she recognised Goldie's hand. She pulled out the letter and began reading.

'Dear Stephanie,

The usual blast about toll calls from the accounts section, so am dutifully trying to cut costs. To the point. I want you to go to Mount Cook next week (I'm laughing at the accounts section!). Seriously, that's the one place where you can find an international celebrity, writer and film producer travelling under the name of Sam Rinde. I've been in touch with him and his office suggested he might do one interview, but at his convenience only. He's flying immediately to Mount Cook—so start packing! He hasn't given any interviews for three years, the last being at the premiere of one of his films, so I'm being optimistic.

'Rumour says he's here because he's thinking of doing a film on an avalanche tragedy. With the interest in New Zealand films, you can guess his mere presence here sparks speculation.

'I don't need to tell you to wear kid gloves when dealing with him. As far as everyone else is concerned, you're simply going to Mount Cook on holiday. Apart from the man himself, I expect you can cover your visit with interviews with staff from the Park on the growth of tourism in the area, the attraction of Mount Cook and possibly a history of famous climbs in the area. (Then I won't get too much of a blast from accounts!) However, you're going there to get one interview as far as I'm concerned, the rest is a little icing on the cake, or should I say snow on the mountain!

'You may prefer to drive down rather than fly, but

use your own initiative. Book your motel through Glencoe Lodge where he's staying. Apparently he prefers the privacy of motels to hotels. I'll enclose a list of several questions I'd like you to ask, but again use your own judgment. Enjoy pre-recording your programme!

'Have a nice time,

Goldie.'

Stephanie put down the letter thoughtfully and picked up the accompanying sheet, a brief résumé of the man's career, a sketchy biography, and the dates at Mount Cook. His private life was remarkably private, she thought.

Studying her schedule for the following week, she groaned. It was all very well for Goldie to calmly order her to Mount Cook. It would be a joy, but she still had the programme to organise and pre-record before she left.

Hastily she studied the man's schedule. She decided to drive down on Wednesday after her programme was completed. It was an easy road all the way to Mount Cook and driving was something she found pleasant. She could settle in that night and the next day try to meet her subject. With luck she could possibly do the interview immediately, then she could relax, but if not she would have a few days up her sleeve.

At least, she thought with a smile, Mount Cook would be a long distance from Dare Nayton!

CHAPTER EIGHT

STEPHANIE booked a call to Mount Cook to check on accommodation and ordered a motel for four nights, then began replanning her own schedule. The studio was free on the Saturday and she pencilled in her times, then went to her office to begin telephoning.

So much for her lazy weekend, she thought. Before she left that evening she had re-scheduled all of the interviews and had managed to complete two. She knew that for the next few days life would be busy, but at least she would have time for herself at Mount Cook. Providing, she reminded herself, she could get the interview easily.

That thought was uppermost in her mind as Stephanie took the road to Mount Cook. She had left behind the programmes and the work until the weekend and set off with a feeling of eager anticipation.

The scenery was familiar until she reached Geraldine, and the rich lushness of the hills after the dryness of the plains formed a striking change. The trees and the crops made it seem like a different country. As the road led inland and the countryside changed again, she found herself looking towards the mountains, beginning to name them as she had as a child on similar jaunts. The last time she had been this way had been five years before, with the family and Dare. They had stopped at Lake Tekapo for a skiing holiday.

She filled the car up with petrol, checked her map for

distances and walked around for five minutes, once she reached the Lake. The sight of the blue waters up to the mountains, white peaks against the sky, was magnificent. She felt the peace of the scene steal into her, despite the few people around. Absently she wandered down to the shore line, then smiled as she saw the bronze dog, a monument erected by the run holders. Dare had read the Gaelic '*Beannachdan air na Cu Caorach*', translating it 'Blessings on the Sheepdog', on their last visit. She could remember him sketching it, and now she remembered how his eyes had gone to the mountains at the head of the lake and he had told her that one day he would paint them. Together they had crossed over to the little stone chapel, its view more beautiful than any stained glass window could ever be. Hand in hand they had looked at each other and looked through the clear glass past the cross to the lake and the mountains.

A bus pulled up noisily with a hiss of compression and a gaggle of tourists scattered. Stephanie went back to her car. She would press on to Lake Pukaki; at least there she would find no memories of Dare.

The car purred along on the almost empty roads. The conditions, thought Stephanie, could hardly be more perfect. The sun was beginning to set as she headed up the side of Lake Pukaki. She noted the changes that the hydro power schemes had caused. Trees had been planted by their thousands and although the canals seemed stiff and artificial, Stephanie had to admit to a feeling of approval in a job skilfully done. The briar roses seemed to have remained unaffected by the changes around them, the pink and white of their flowers glowing in the softening light.

The mountains were almost surrounding her now and

every so often she caught breathtaking views. Once or twice she stopped the car simply to gaze at the snow-topped giants. A glance at her watch reminded her that the time was fast disappearing, and she put her foot down to the accelerator, wanting to be at the Lodge before losing all the sun. She shivered as she pulled into the motel.

The warmth of the reception was reassuring. Guided to a motel, Stephanie admired the layout of the units, ensuring privacy for the guests. Her car had its own shelter from the snow and the porch formed an entrance to her unit. There were four units in her block and the positioning of the other blocks ensured that each had their own views out to the mountains. Her own had a large sliding door on to a terrace adjoining the neighbouring unit. She decided that she would sit there to eat her dinner. The motel boasted an excellent cooker, and as she unpacked her supplies and her wardrobe she began singing.

The precious tapes and recorder she put in her bedroom, then she locked the unit and went for a walk. It was becoming increasingly dark, but the last faint hint of sunlight played around the scene. They were in a hollow carved from the mountains millions of years earlier. The almost flat-plain contrasted with the giant mountain ahead of her, and she found her eyes drawn to its three peaks. The silence around her had its own beauty. The trees and scrubby sub-alpine vegetation delighted her.

One or two people passed her on the path, but they were just as keen to appreciate the solitude she had found. She moved on slowly, finding the signposts to the garage, the Hermitage, the Post Office, the ranger station and the school. Ignoring them, she kept up her solitary meandering along the path. Some thoughtful person had placed a sturdy seat just off the path, and Stephanie sat down, watching the sunlight play on the mountains.

As she sat in the gathering dark a faint familiar noise startled her. It sounded for all the world like someone sketching. She frowned and blamed her over-active imagination.

The last rays were highlighting the clouds, and she gasped in wonder as the whole snow-covered tops blazed pink for a few fleeting moments. The splendour was timeless. Stephanie knew that as long as she lived she would never forget it. The mountain had been almost free of clouds for that last glow, and she remembered the Maori name for it, Aorangi, the cloud-piercer. It was, she felt, singularly appropriate. Amongst the lofty Alps it reached just that little further to split the clouds which usually lay on top of its peaks.

Slowly Stephanie became aware of some other person just behind the tree, half hidden by the scrubby plants. In the deepening gloom the atmosphere swung suddenly like a mist on the mountain to nape prickling fear. She gripped the edge of the seat, suddenly wishing she had a torch to dispel her fears.

'You—here?' The voice was like dark velvet and as familiar as her own.

'Dare!' Stephanie heard the astonishment in her answer. 'What on earth are you doing here?'

'Looking at the mountains.' His answer was dry. 'What about you?'

'Work.'

'Work? Don't tell me you suddenly decided to interview the head ranger and had to come all the way here to do it?'

'Very well, I won't, then,' Stephanie answered sweetly

In the dark she was aware of the swift look Dare gave her.

'I was intending to go along to the Hermitage and have a drink when I finished. You might as well join me.'

It was hardly a gracious invitation. Despite an instinctive desire to turn him down with as much of a squelch as she could muster, Stephanie realised that his escort would be a perfect cover for her.

'Thank you,' she said sweetly.

They walked along the path, glad of the light shining the way. The bulk of the large building of the hotel reared ahead of them, its lights welcoming. The admonition above the door to remove ski and tramping boots made Stephanie smile. The candlelit restaurant on one side was occupied by a few diners but there was merriment coming from the small bar on the other side of the entry. Dare led the way, totally at ease in the cosmopolitan surroundings. He seated Stephanie at a small table and went to get their drinks while Stephanie looked around her. In one corner a group of tourists were reliving hilarious tales and in the middle another party were discussing the different faces of Mount Cook. Not far from Stephanie was an older man who seemed to be quietly observing the scene. She looked at him again, wondering if he was Sam Rinde.

'Stop staring at the man. He's too old for you,' Dare said the words softly as he put the drinks on the table. He placed his sketchbook like a fence separating them from the solitary figure.

'I thought he was someone I should know,' she said softly.

'Don't try that old line!' he snorted. He downed his drink quickly, as though she had irritated him beyond endurance.

'Can I see your sketch of the sunset on the mountain, please, Dare?'

To her surprise he agreed and placed the book on the table. His hand touched hers as he turned the pages and a thrill like an electric shock shot through her. She moved back swiftly, as Dare propped the block so she could see it.

'That's good, Dare,' she breathed as she studied the page.

The dim light of the cocktail bar was hardly the best place to view the scene, but despite that the bold outline of the mountain held a fascination.

'I'll block this in here,' explained Dare, 'and see if I can get that shadow and light effect across this angle. I doubt if I'd ever be able to come close to getting that colour, though.'

'You'll manage it. Look at the exact shading you selected for the butterfly.'

'Overdone, too vivid, unreal!' he mocked.

'You know I didn't mean that. I was just angry with you.'

Dare's eyes met hers, and she felt the magnetism between them glow like sunlight on the snow. She looked back at the sketch, then Dare turned the page back to one he must have done earlier with the motel unit silhouetted against the backdrop of the mountains.

'Just for my personal record,' he grinned.

'It looks like my unit,' said Stephanie. 'I suppose they all look alike.'

'I'm in number forty-six.'

She looked at him bleakly. 'I'm your next door neighbour.' She took her key with its large tag and put it on the table.

Another group of tourists arriving caused the man beside them to shift up, and automatically Stephanie pocketed her key.

'Guess I'm another neighbour,' he said with a smile. 'Sam K. Rinde.'

Dare introduced Stephanie and himself and the man disarmed them completely by saying he had been curious about the sketch. Stephanie was relieved he seemed so pleasant and invited him to join them. She wanted to tell him immediately about the interview, but there were too many listeners in the crowded bar. At least, she told herself, she could pop along to his motel and explain later.

'That's really good. I'd like to see more of your work. Got any here?' Sam Rinde commented, as he handed back the sketch block.

'No. I'm travelling light this trip,' put in Dare.

'I know the feeling. Where are you from?'

Stephanie sat back as the two men conversed. She had the feeling Dare was not too pleased at their interruption, but for herself it was a wonderful opportunity to get to know Mr Rinde better. He played the part of the tourist perfectly, she admitted.

'What do you know about the trip up the Tasman Glacier?'

Stephanie realised that both men were looking at her for an answer and rapidly replayed the question.

'Almost nothing. I think you can fly up or go part of the way by car, or there's a bus trip. I thought of . . .' She stopped, aware she was about to say 'interviewing the driver', and hastily substituted, 'possibly going on the bus tour tomorrow.'

'Think I might join you, if I may.'

'That would be fine. What do you think you'll do, Dare?'

'I think I'd better take that trip too,' he said quietly.

Stephanie hastily took another drink, hiding a grin as she realised that Dare thought she had arranged the suggestion as a way of getting to know Mr Rinde better.

'Let me buy you two a drink,' offered Sam Rinde.

'Some other time.' Dare stood up. 'I've come a long way today.'

Stephanie found her arm gently but firmly tucked into Dare's and willy-nilly forced to her feet. Short of forcibly detaching herself and making a scene, she knew she would have to go with him.

'We'll meet again,' she promised Mr Rinde as Dare led the way out of the crowded bar. Once outside Dare dropped her arm like a hot potato and she felt hurt that once they were on their own he should revert to his earlier antagonism. All the same she was glad of his escort as they made their way down the dark paths toward the motels. The silence between them seemed magnified by the looming presence of the mountains and the brilliance of the stars. Moonlight only etched the difference more clearly.

When they reached the motel Dare saw her politely to her door before turning to his adjoining unit. Stephanie wondered how she had not recognised his car in the garage next to hers. From Dare's point of view it would look as though she had deliberately set out to follow him.

Sighing, Stephanie began preparing a meal. The motel unit was well equipped and she had stocked the fridge with meat and groceries she had bought. She could hear similar sounds from Dare's unit and wondered what he was cooking. It seemed ridiculous to be cooking for herself when she might as well be doing it for Dare as well, but he had not suggested their sharing a meal and she didn't want to antagonise him further. Probably, she realised, he was waiting for her to run in with some of the delicious savoury she had concocted.

'Well, he'll have a jolly long wait!' She glared at the pots and pans. She switched on the radio, then flicked it off again on hearing the poor reception. She looked at the food she had prepared, then heard a step on the motel on the other side. On inspiration she decided she could offer Mr Rinde the meal and explain her presence at the same time.

Without stopping to think she ran along the adjoining patio and knocked at the door. Quite obviously the man was surprised to see her, and even more surprised when she told him her identity.

'Right, so long as you can guarantee you're a reasonable cook, young lady, I'd love to share dinner with you.'

He followed her along to her motel and slid the door shut.

'Now, let's just talk. I've no intention of giving an interview until I get to know you a little better.'

'It's meant to be the other way around,' laughed Stephanie.

Over dinner she found it remarkably easy to talk to the producer. His tales of film-making were spellbinding and Stephanie found her laughter ringing out several times. By the time he had helped her clear the dishes and tidied the main room again, both felt they had found a friend. It was late when the producer finally went back to his own motel. Stephanie found it difficult to slide the door completely shut, the last half inch was jammed. Deciding that she was probably perfectly safe to leave the door in that position, she prepared for bed.

Suddenly the day's events and the long drive seemed to have caught up with her, and she climbed into bed with pleasure. Almost immediately she switched off her light, punched the unfamiliar pillows into a suitable shape and settled to sleep.

An icy cold draught awoke her. Stumbling, she crashed into the table, before switching on the light. It was the main light and it enabled her to see a small stone blocking the door's runner. Picking it up, she flung it far into the darkness and shut the door. A glance at her watch revealed that it was almost four o'clock.

Shivering, Stephanie huddled into bed, but sleep seemed far away. She went into the kitchen and made a hot drink, then took it back to bed. On the small table were a pile of brochures inviting her to fly up to the West Coast glaciers from Mount Cook airport or to fly to Milford Sound. Another gave details of the Tasman Glacier and the coach tour times. She read it, then found her warmth restored and sleep softly descending again. She pulled the covers over her head instinctively to block off the light, then snuggled down again.

When she woke there was just time for a hasty breakfast before joining the other tourists waiting for the bus. She was greeted by Sam Rinde, and she smiled at his dark glasses and floppy hat which proved an effective disguise.

'No sign of your friend?' he asked.

'Dare? Guess he must have changed his mind,' Stephanie answered as she boarded the bus. 'Now I've time to think, his car wasn't outside his unit this morning.'

Her thoughts were still on the whereabouts of Dare

when the bus lurched forward.

'The driver seems to know his subject,' commented the producer as the history of the region unfolded.

Stephanie found herself listening with interest, and only as the bus stopped did she wonder why she had thought geography a dull subject at school. She followed as the others began climbing up the side of the shingle-clad slope at Husky Point to get a better view. The wind was very strong and she shivered as they climbed in single file. Her view was restricted by the man in front and she wished Dare was with her, she would have felt a lot safer. The path opened and they stood triumphantly on a narrow point, looking directly at the great glacier and the towering peaks.

'Come over here out of the wind.'

The advice was sensible and Stephanie turned to obey willingly. As suggested, she could now view the snowy river of ice and shingle without the blast of the wind. The impressive sight of the mountains rearing up around her was spine-tingling in its awesomeness.

'There's your friend,' gestured the producer. 'Guess he decided to get an early start.'

Stephanie could see Dare had set up his gear on a similar point not far away. He appeared to be totally engrossed in his work, but she knew with instinctive pain that he was just as aware of their party as if he was with them. As if to emphasise the point he stood up, his face as hard as the rocks around him. Stephanie looked at the terrain which separated them. The gulf appeared to her untrained eye to be difficult to climb. It seemed to epitomise the distance between them.

Yesterday Dare had been pleasant, they had parted

more or less on good terms, so why this ice-like anger? Stephanie wondered. She flinched from the glance Dare flung at her. From that look it seemed as if he wished her under the mountain of shingle that formed the lower part of the glacier's cover.

'The driver's waiting for you, Stephanie.'

Numbly she turned and negotiated the tricky path downwards. A lonely fragile flower bloomed in a crack of the rock where she had been standing. She marvelled that the tiny seed could have found the heart to grow in such an inhospitable place. It was ridiculous, but it seemed like an omen of good luck. Surely if such a flower could grow there, her love for Dare would blossom too.

Stephanie rounded the corner into the face of the gale. Stepping carefully, she felt almost lighthearted, seeing the majesty and beauty around her as a part of a glorious morning. By the time she was back on board the bus she felt as though she was able to wave flags from the top of Mount Cook, but as the bus progressed back to the hotel her spirits suddenly dropped. She had forgotten Barbara. It wasn't enough that this chance encounter would give her a time to explain the tangled mess to Dare, there was his love for the dazzling blonde.

Absently she noted that the driver must be one of the people she put on her interview list. His skill as a raconteur would be perfect on radio. It reminded her that she still had to arrange a time with Sam Rinde. He seemed friendly last night, but each time she had mentioned the interview he had put her off. Now she wanted to finalise a time so she could leave as quickly as possible.

'Mr Rinde, would you give me the interview this afternoon, perhaps after lunch?' she asked.

'Sorry, I've arranged a flight up to the top to take a look around. I don't really want to answer your questions until I've been up there again. I flew over to the Milford Sound yesterday—now that's remarkable, all those waterfalls gushing everywhere.'

'You're sidetracking me,' smiled Stephanie.

'Was I?' answered the producer with an amiable smile. 'Tell you what, have dinner with me tonight, then I'll give you the interview afterwards.'

'That will be lovely!'

Stephanie waved goodbye as she went into her own unit. It had all been so incredibly easy she could hardly believe her good fortune. So much for Goldie's dire warnings, she thought. With the rest of the day free she could begin the series of other topics.

She was just coming back from interviewing the head ranger when she met Dare. Automatically they fell into step together as they reached the motels.

'You don't waste time, do you?' Dare shot out with icy contempt.

'What do you mean? With work?' Genuinely puzzled, Stephanie put a hand on his arm. Almost roughly he shrugged it off.

'I'll never be able to understand you, Stephanie. Why did you have to pick up that guy? Couldn't you do without it for one night?'

He strode away, leaving an almost paralysed Stephanie behind. She raced after him once the full import of his words had sunk in. Hammering on his door, she called out his name.

'Dare! I demand to see you!'

He flung open the door, and she faltered, seeing the

blazing expression on his face. Then her own anger boosted her and she stepped forward.

'I think it's time we got this sorted out, Dare. Number one, I did not pick up Mr Rinde. You introduced me yourself, remember. Number two, he's a fascinating man, who's travelled extensively, and he's charming, courteous and kind. Virtues you could well copy!'

'Don't you lecture me!' Dare almost pulled her into the motel and shut the door. 'Did you or did you not entertain your new acquaintance last night?' he demanded.

Stephanie pushed a hand through her hair. 'I had him in for dinner.'

Dare's glance went through her, nailing her to the floor. 'And dinner goes on till four in the morning? I heard you shutting the door. The noise woke me up. At least you could have been a little more discreet!'

'You're impossible!' Stephanie sobbed in anger and anguish. 'If you were that conscious of what I was doing you would have heard him leave at ten o'clock. At four I woke up because I was cold. The door had stuck the night before and I was too tired to notice that a tiny stone had jammed it. It was a different story at four in the morning.' She glared at him. 'You must have heard Sam leave at ten o'clock. We stood on the patio that joins the units.'

Dare looked at her thoughtfully. 'It's possible, it's even plausible. You heard me go out about a quarter to ten for a walk, I suppose. When I returned all was quiet and I presumed you'd gone to bed. Then at four o'clock I began to realise what a fool I'd been.'

'You don't believe me, do you?' Stephanie put in. 'You painted me scarlet, and you refuse to consider that you could ever have made a mistake!'

She turned and walked out of the unit, closing the door behind her. Sadly she went back to her own unit and let the sobs ease their way from her burning heart. It seemed as though everything she did was bound to be misconstrued. She flung herself down on the bed and buried her head in the softness of the pillow.

'Stephanie, don't cry, please.'

She turned on hearing his voice. He must have followed her.

'Go away,' she said, her muffled voice indistinct in the pillow.

He gathered her quivering body, holding it firmly against his until the tears stilled on the edges of her lashes.

'I'm sorry, Stephanie,' he murmured, 'I guess I was wrong.'

He kissed each eyelid gently, brushing away the tear as he did so. Stephanie sniffed inelegantly and Dare smiled at her tenderly.

'That's better. Now I promise to listen. It's six-thirty and we can talk all night if necessary.' He leant a casual arm around her and bent to kiss her mouth, a light touch which sent tremors racing through her. Stephanie felt completely overwhelmed. It was such a reversal of their usual fights that she sat up and stared at him. He smiled at the expression on her face.

'Are you trying to tell me you should be painted white, or even cream?' he said softly.

'Oh, Dare! You mean you want to know the whole story? Here? Now?'

'Right here. Right now. If you want to tell me, of course.'

Stephanie frowned, wondering how to begin. She found

it very distracting with Dare's arm around her waist and his mouth only inches from her own. She tried to collect her straggling thoughts, desperate to remember events in their sequence. Time was so important. A thought suddenly disturbed her.

'What did you say the time was? Oh, help! I promised to have dinner with Sam Rinde.'

Dare sat up as if he had been struck and she could almost see the harsh lines cut into the planes of his face.

'Please, Dare, believe me! I know it sounds odd, but I've got to have dinner with Sam Rinde—I promised.'

'I'll see you after, then.' Dare stood up, but his face looked hard and cold. 'Spare me the time, if you can explain.'

Stephanie faltered. 'Do you mind waiting a little while, after dinner? I'm not sure how long I'll be.'

'Until ten o'clock, then that's it,' Dare said quietly, his look ominous, as he left the motel.

She suddenly realised that she could hardly go into one of the most select restaurants in the whole country looking like a windblown seed from the mountains. Hastily she pulled out a gold and red silk dinner gown which had a demure front and the shoes in red and gold to match it. Her shower took only a few moments and she wound her hair up deftly, plaiting it into a side effect on the crown. The gown took only moments to slip into, and as she smoothed it into place she viewed her appearance with anxiety. Her watch being silver looked wrong, so she removed it and put on her gold bracelet.

A knock on the door a few seconds later told her she had no longer, and she opened the door to smile at Mr Rinde.

'Hey, you look a knockout! Now don't tell me you

always wanted to be a movie star.' He offered her his arm gallantly.

'No, I'll stick to radio, though I wouldn't mind the production side of television. That would be fascinating.'

'Hair-raising! It's a voracious monster.'

Stephanie made a mental note of his reply for her interview. Throughout dinner she was conscious that she was being interviewed herself. That knowledge only added spice to the dinner and kept her thoughts from straying to Dare. Dinner was leisurely in style and the service discreet, and she would have enjoyed it enormously if she was not quite so conscious of the time. Her host was in a leisurely mood. After dinner he sat over coffee and liqueurs for what appeared to an alarmed Stephanie to be an inordinate length of time. It was with relief that she at last collected her recorder and notes from her motel.

The light in Dare's suite was showing. She could not afford to rush such an important interview, yet that was exactly what she felt like doing. It even crossed her mind to tell Sam Rinde about the whole affair so that he would know she had to leave at ten, but regretfully she decided that would be totally unprofessional.

She put it out of her mind and set up the recorder. She knew that if she treated it more as a conversation Sam Rinde was far more likely to relax and give more interesting detail. So it proved. Once or twice she had to switch off the recorder on his signal, but it was easy to pick up a similar thread. When she changed the tape he merely raised his eyebrows in surprise, but agreed to carry on.

Stephanie could feel her excitement rising. She knew that by some miracle she had reached a perfect accord with Sam Rinde. Selecting another facet of his work was rather like turning a perfectly cut diamond in the sunlight. Sam Rinde seemed to be enjoying it too, and he spontaneously suggested other angles, seeing her programme from his own insight. They found themselves totally engrossed. His stories were in perfect radio style, his experiences were laced with adventure and exotic places and his observations on some of the people he had worked with were often brilliantly funny.

A couple of times when she changed a tape Stephanie glanced at the clock on the wall, but was reassured. They finished on an absurdly funny incident which had Stephanie almost in tears from laughter. Weakly she packed her gear and thanked Sam Rinde.

'I'll see you in the morning,' he promised.

'I'll look forward to it,' she agreed lightheartedly. She slipped along to her unit and put down the precious tapes and the recorder. Aware suddenly of feeling tired, she looked anxiously at her appearance in the mirror. Would the scarlet dress give rise to yet another painful comment? Quickly she pulled it off and threw on a favourite fluffy sweater and jeans. She strapped on her watch again and automatically noticed the time.

One-fourteen. One-fourteen!

She stopped. Horror gripped her. The watch must be wrong! But its steady flashing told her it was working only too well. She remembered checking the clock in Sam Rinde's unit. She must have made a mistake or else the clock had been running slowly. Her eyes fell on the tapes. Sheer experience should have told her the clock was wrong.

Groaning, she collapsed on the bed. She recalled Dare' bitter phrase, 'Spare me the time, if you can explain! Whatever would he think?

CHAPTER NINE

STEPHANIE looked at her watch again. One-fifteen! Dare would have given her up hours before. He would have taken his own reading from the fact she had spent so long with Sam Rinde. Stephanie swallowed. She wondered if she should go and see Dare and try to explain. But what could she say?

The thought of his anger decided her. It would be bad enough telling him in the morning without adding fuel to the fire by waking him up. At the crack of dawn she could invite him to watch the sunrise on the mountains. She hesitated, wondering how he would view such an invitation. She could imagine Dare's reaction! No. She would just tell the plain truth. Dare would listen. She should have explained about Sam Rinde earlier. She owed Dare that much.

Slowly she changed into her pyjamas and climbed into bed. Hefting the recorder and tapes beside her, along with papers, pencil and a clipboard, she settled herself comfortably if perilously for some of the items. At least she could fill in the intervening hours by checking the tapes. She knew she wouldn't sleep.

She plugged in the headphones and switched on. Silence puzzled her and she sat up straighter and looked at the sound level. Deftly she turned up the volume control a little, and then in sheer desperation right up. Still the tape ground on. Stephanie looked at it disbelievingly. Common sense reminded her that she had checked the levels frequently when recording, and to further reassure her the needle was wavering slightly on the voice levels indicator.

She unplugged the headphones and the voice leapt at her, a deep booming laugh which just about blew her out of bed. Fumbling for the volume control, she knocked the recorder and the whole lot of papers, tape boxes and machine went crashing.

A second later she managed to switch off the voice and survey the scene. Guiltily she hoped she had not woken up Dare next door. If his unit was the reverse of hers, his bed would be just through the wall. The walls were designed to keep out noise, but no architect would have dreamt of a sound of so many decibels being used. Stephanie's ears still thrummed with the noise. She rubbed them as she picked up the machine and the papers. Turning the machine on, she checked that the recorder and the tape were undamaged. To her relief the voice spoke as normally as when she had recorded it. Hastily she unwound the tape and put it in its box. She didn't want to risk any more disasters.

As she lay in bed Stephanie wondered about continuing her stay at Mount Cook. Once she had straightened the situation with Dare everything would be wonderful. He could go on painting while she recorded the chief ranger and one or two of the staff. She could arrange an interview with the bus driver immediately after lunch and then she could drive back to town, but it seemed a pity not to explore further, especially if Dare would accompany her. The sights of the Tasman Glacier had been so spectacular. She picked up the brochures again and saw one recommending various walks. The sound of Sealy Tarns and the

Blue Lakes as well as the mighty Hooker and Meuller Glaciers convinced her. There could well be enough programme material to keep her working twenty-four hours a day for a whole month.

Stephanie cuddled under the blankets. For the first time she allowed herself to think of the tender way Dare had kissed her. It had been as gentle and as surprising as the delicate white flower she had seen among the snow and rocks of the mountain. Until, she reminded herself, he had realised that she was going out with Sam Rinde. Stephanie sighed, wishing again that she had explained to Dare why her meeting with Sam Rinde was so important.

Sun was dazzling on the snow on the heights when she woke. She took a moment to recall the facts of the previous night, then she leapt out of bed. She had to reach Dare before he left.

Dare must be trusted; he would understand her predicament. She showered hastily. It would be all right, she told herself. She turned the tap the wrong way and the shower of cold water made her shiver. It reminded her of reality. It told her Dare loved Barbara. Swiftly she flung on her clothes and applied the merest dash of lipstick. Why, why hadn't she woken earlier!

She ran to his unit, using the connecting patio. He had left the curtain pulled back and she could see at a glance that he was not there. Her heart sank. Hammering on the door, she called out his name, but only the slight wind answered her. Slowly she made her way back to her own unit. She forced herself to eat some breakfast, but the food was tasteless.

'I'll see Dare later—at least his gear is still in the unit,' she thought.

A quiet knock on the door made her heart leap. She ran to open it, thinking it was Dare, and felt her face drop when she saw Sam Rinde.

'Thought you might need this.' He handed over a small shining spindle which connected the headphones to the recorder.

'Thanks, Sam. I didn't realise I'd dropped it out. I missed it last night. I hope I didn't wake you.'

'I thought I heard something, but I was too sleepy to care. You know, if all interviewers were like you I wouldn't have got my fierce man image! How do you feel about going for a walk this morning?'

Stephanie nodded. If she couldn't see Dare she might as well go with Sam for a tramp. She might even see Dare when she was out. Hope raised its head again.

'Where are we going?' she asked.

'I checked with a ranger yesterday, and there's a point which is just a comfortable stroll. No mountain climbing needed to get to Kea Point! You'll be back for lunch.'

'Sounds a good idea. I've got a couple of interviews I should do this afternoon.'

'Is your friend able to come with us?' Sam enquired.

'No, Dare's away. I guess he made an early start.'

'I hope he didn't mind me taking you to dinner last night.'

'No, he and I are just old neighbours. Our parents' farms are opposite. It was sheer coincidence he happened to be here,' she told him.

'Then it won't be a problem if I ask you to accompany me this morning?'

'I'd like that very much. Dare's already left. Give me twenty minutes and I'll be organised.'

'That will suit me just fine.'

Once her visitor had left Stephanie hastily made her bed and tidied the unit, then flew over to the reception area to leave messages for the staff she wanted to interview that afternoon.

Dare was just climbing into his car when she went back to the unit. He must have returned for some gear as she saw him place some on the front seat. He caught sight of her and his face went hard and shuttered. Ignoring her, he turned the key and the motor fired immediately.

'Dare—wait, please!' she called.

'Yes?' His gaze flicked her with contempt.

Stephanie felt her explanation dry up in the face of that look. She knew she had to stop him from driving off.

'Dare, I didn't mean to forget, honestly. It was the clock in Sam's unit.' Her voice trailed off under the blistering scorn on Dare's face. The excuse sounded weak even to her.

'Let me explain . . .' she pleaded.

'I've heard enough!' Each word was as sharply cutting as a whip. Stephanie reeled under the intensity. Dare revved the motor and with a swoosh of gravel he was gone.

Stephanie leaned back against the pillar of the porch. She felt as if her body had been squashed, flattened as effectively as if Dare had physically run over her. It was almost like being winded. Gasping for breath, she gradually regained some control, but it took five minutes before her hands stopped shaking.

'You been running? There was no need. The mountains have stood for a long time,' Sam's voice sang out.

Stephanie managed a nod and fell in beside him. It was easier to go with him than to explain. She wasn't even sure she could; her heart felt like a solid block of ice inside her chest.

They stepped out briskly, their eyes looking towards Mount Sefton.

'Your friend mentioned yesterday that there are some remarkable ice faces on the hanging glaciers,' said Sam. 'Apparently they're three or four hundred feet thick.'

Again Stephanie made an effort to nod agreement. She was relieved that Sam saw nothing odd in her silence. Gradually the effort of walking warmed her, thawing her reactions and feelings. The spectacular beauty all around them was so awesome, the mountains' sheer size so splendid, it seeped into her.

'We seem to have the world to ourselves,' commented Sam.

'It's incredible!' breathed Stephanie. 'Listen to the sound of the wind in the grass!' They stopped for a moment to enjoy the delight.

'Just like the sound of the waves of the sea,' commented Sam.

The grasses changed character and they passed a clump of late foxgloves and the seed spikes of alpine flora. Stephanie recognised the remains of the yellow Poor Man's Tobacco. As they began climbing the vegetation changed again and she was able to point out to Sam the patch of alpine ranunculus, half hidden among the rocks and scrub.

'Wrong time for the white flower, I'm afraid. It's rather distinctive, most people call it the Mount Cook Lily.'

'Never mind.' Sam pointed. 'There's a plant I recognise as one your friend sketched—the big daisy over there.' He had a butterfly on it too. Quite a number of the little blue ones and those fingernail size, orange ones with the black edge around here,' he added.

Stephanie had found the little butterflies charming, but they had already reminded her of the opinion Dare had of her. A fantail darted out of a tree and delighted them with its mid-air acrobatics. Its flash of white feathers as its fan-like tail opened and shut made them both smile.

They scrambled around the boulders that had been left by earlier glaciers and climbed the last section of the track, moving through bush and rocks. A moment later they reached the outlook. Sitting quietly at an easel was a long lean figure.

'Dare!' The name came out like a squeak as the air suddenly disappeared from Stephanie's lungs. A pair of ice-blue eyes met hers.

Dare was a man of many parts and as difficult to know as the mountains around them. It was obvious that he had no intention of ever allowing a certain Stephanie Fernley near him again.

Sam Rinde approached him with an open smile. 'You were at the motel earlier. How did you beat us here?'

'A road cuts off half the distance,' Dare spoke shortly.

'Say, that's impressive!' Sam was openly admiring Dare's work. Stephanie waited for the explosion of wrath, but Dare was silent.

'Guess we'd better turn back,' Sam added. 'Stephanie has an interview to do. This girl never stops working. She's hardly had a minute to herself since she arrived.'

Dare shot a glance at Stephanie. 'Couldn't have phrased it better myself,' he muttered sotto voce. Hurt, Stephanie could only gaze at him.

'I'll just go down to the part where the track splits.' Sam smiled at Stephanie. 'Catch me up in a few minutes.'

Stephanie thanked him silently. She wondered how Sam could have possibly known how desperately she wanted to talk to Dare. The wind blew coldly, iced from the snow around the mountains.

'Dare, I must talk to you,' she spoke urgently.

Dare cast her a look and then studied his work. His dismissal was so calculated Stephanie held on to a nearby tree for comfort. She couldn't allow him to think of her so bitterly.

'Please, Dare, I want to explain.'

He stood up. His attitude was so fierce she took an involuntary step back.

'Explanations are not necessary,' he grated.

Stephanie knew she had left it too late. Dare had judged and condemned her. She could argue no longer; her fight had been knocked out of her by the savage intensity of Dare's expression. She turned away and began climbing down the track. She didn't see the trees or the rocks that she scrambled over automatically. All she was conscious of was the desire to flee. It was almost a shock to see Sam ahead of her at the turn-off. Stephanie found her numbed body beginning to react again as they crossed the shingle fans left by the past glaciers. Even so, she was glad that Sam didn't attempt to make conversation until their path brought them out by the Hermitage.

'Come and have lunch with me, Stephanie?' he invited.

'Sorry, Sam, I've got an interview to do in ten minutes,' she said, glancing at her watch. 'Thanks all the same.'

She headed back to the motel. She had been glad of the excuse. She didn't feel like eating ever again.

Work kept her occupied all afternoon, but she found her concentration more difficult than usual. When she had finished her last interview one of the staff escorted her to the Hermitage bar for a drink. She found herself amidst other off-duty staff and found her spirits rising in their company. One had a birthday to celebrate and called for champagne. Stephanie was given a glassful, and she toasted the young man with a bright smile. No one would ever guess, she thought sombrely, that she had a broken heart. Her face pulled into a lugubrious expression. Dare Nayton's opinion would not affect her, not one little bit. She had work and she enjoyed it!

Her hand curled round the stem of the glass and she watched the bubbles form a star. Looking up, she saw Dare enter the room. Instantly their eyes met. His slowly travelled over her, then looked at the group of men she was surrounded by, and an expressive look of distaste curled his lips. Stephanie gulped on her champagne. She wanted to get out. She smiled at the young man who had poured her drink.

'Would you mind carrying my gear back to my motel?'

'Not at all.'

Stephanie said her farewells, then, escorted by the young man, left the bar. She tried not to look at Dare as she walked past him, but the temptation was irresistible. Dare Nayton could paint her not only scarlet bat pulsating, fluorescent pink as well!

Once she reached the motel she said goodnight to the young officer, then ran through the work she had completed. She was astonished to find she was hungry and she cooked up a meal, her mind occupied with the tape. There was a bleak satisfaction in knowing that she had done even better with her interviews than she had dreamed. She opened the sliding door and watched the late sunlight make the mountain tops turn pink, then the darkling sky covered them. Wearily she prepared for bed.

The alarm clock woke her from a sound sleep. As awareness penetrated she sat up, then walked to the window. The sun was just outlining the tops of the mountains, the rainbow of colours telling her it was to be a good day. She had made up her mind that she would return to Christchurch that day; it was just too uncomfortable living next door to Dare Nayton. She dressed for the trip and packed her suitcase. As she put it in the car she saw Sam Rinde leave his unit.

'Just coming to see you, lass,' he greeted her. 'I'm off to Queenstown this morning. My flight goes in an hour, but I have to get down to the airstrip.'

'I decided I'd better get back to work, too, Sam. Listen, I can take you to the airport. I'll be going past and I'm almost ready.'

'Then I'll accept. I'll get my bag.'

They were just putting Sam's suitcase in the car when Dare left his unit. Instinctively Stephanie looked at him, hoping for some sign that he had changed his mind. His long lean figure looked part of the mountain scene; he belonged, she thought sadly. For a moment she felt hope rise in her heart as he turned towards her—but then Sam stood up and Stephanie saw the hateful expression smoulder in Dare's eyes. He strode past, heading for the little Post Office on the rise behind them.

She gave in her keys and paid at the reception area and collected the receipts from the accounts section. She couldn't leave fast enough. She wanted to be away before seeing Dare Nayton again.

Within minutes they were on their way to the nearby airport. Sam Rinde kept her entertained on their way, with hair-raising tales about luggage. She dropped him off with the feeling that she had made a good friend, and she was delighted when he told her he would probably call in to see her in Christchurch before he left the country.

Thinking back to her concern over meeting Sam Rinde, she could smile. He had been so delightfully easy to interview that she was surprised at his reputation for eating journalists for breakfast. Perhaps the treatment at the Hermitage and the motels had pleased him. As she was musing she glanced down at her petrol gauge and uttered a horrified gasp. She had been so upset by Dare that she had forgotten to buy petrol before she left Mount Cook! Slackening her foot from the accelerator, she decreased speed, as she calculated the distance ahead of her. The lake beside her and the barren hillsides with the backdrop of the mountains no longer seemed such a beautiful sight. She decided that if a fairy godmother appeared she would know what to ask for immediately.

'I suppose if the worst happens a passing motorist will give me a little, or I can get a ride to the nearest town,' she thought. With the way her luck was running it would be Dare who happened along to see her sitting helplessly by the roadside, miles from anywhere.

With his opinion of her he would probably drive on past, leaving her sitting stranded. But even as she checked the gauge again and saw how dangerously close the needle was to the empty sign she knew that no matter how angry he would be, he would still stop.

She tried to recall the road ahead to see whether she could avoid any great changes in speed. At least she didn't have to worry about traffic, she told herself. There simply wasn't any. The lakeside seemed to go on for ever and she had plenty of time to take in, though not appreciate, the scenery. She began counting the miles as they ticked past and when she reached the last one she began smiling. Although the gauge was showing empty the car kept running, and it wasn't until she pulled up with a smile as white as the mountains that the motor coughed and spluttered.

'Sure timed that right,' commented the petrol pump attendant. 'You should take a ticket in the Kiwi Lottery!'

'I might do just that,' laughed Stephanie. 'I've been nursing it for miles, but I didn't dare dream I'd make it.'

Stephanie heard another car, and automatically she watched as it sped by. Dare hadn't seen her, she thought gratefully. She was profoundly glad she had managed to get to the petrol pumps without his assistance.

'Are you lucky in love, too?' questioned the man.

Stephanie was glad she was saved from making a reply as she bent to get some money from her purse.

Once or twice on the way home she stopped to have a walk around and a meal. She didn't mind the long trip, it helped lessen the pain of knowing Dare and she were farther apart than ever. She wondered what Dare had thought when he saw her drive off with Sam Rinde. Not that she was simply dropping him off at the airport a couple of miles down the road, she guessed.

She felt tired when she pulled up at the familiar flat. She put a call through to Goldie, and his pleasure at her success made her feel considerably better. At least Goldie was always the same, she thought, as she crawled into bed and pulled the blanket close—not like Dare Nayton, painting her white one moment and red the next.

Rain washed the streets black as Stephanie made her way to work the next day. Almost the first person to greet her was Ray and he invited her round for dinner that evening. It reminded Stephanie that she still had a lot of work to do for the party that weekend.

'I'd love to come, Ray, but I'll probably have to leave early. I've quite a bit to do.'

'Was the rumour right? Did you go to Mount Cook to meet someone special? I should warn you that Mat was talking to your mother earlier in the week and we know that a certain well-known artist was to be sketching in the area.'

'Dare was there, but when I went I wasn't aware of that, Ray. I went to interview an incognito film producer and writer who was there on holiday.'

'Wow! Did you manage to get an interview?'

'Two tapes full.'

'Well, you'll be the golden-haired girl this morning. That explains the secrecy. And did you see your friend?' enquired Ray with a hint of a smile.

'Yes, I saw him. We ended up in motel units side by side. And he thought I was with the producer.'

'Only you could do that,' sighed Ray. 'That poor guy!'

'Poor guy, my foot!' snapped Stephanie. 'He puts one and one together . . .'

'And makes two?' put in Ray. 'There's your phone, I'll look forward to all the details tonight.'

Stephanie picked up the phone and answered with her

normal style. She dealt with the minor query, then rang her mother.

'Darling, how lovely for you that Dare was at Mount Cook too. I suppose you spent a lot of time together. Barbara was just saying it was a coincidence. She's been here helping me with the party preparations.'

'Barbara has? That's kind of her.'

'She's a lovely girl, Stephanie. We get on so well together. Alan took her fishing yesterday, to give her a break. She's out helping your father round up the sheep at the moment, and then she's going to town with Olivia. They might call in to see you after shopping.'

'Sorry, Mum, some other time, tell Aunt Olivia. I've promised I'd go straight after work to Ray and Mat's.'

Stephanie thanked her lucky stars she had a reasonable excuse. She just didn't feel like entertaining the wonderful Barbara, in fact she was surprised at the emotions she felt. It couldn't be jealousy, she told herself; she liked Barbara. A mental picture of the other girl and Dare convinced her, and she amended her thoughts. She *was* jealous!

'Barbara's looking forward to the party,' her mother went on. 'I've told her she must come even if Dare doesn't make it.'

Hope leapt for Stephanie. If Dare was still away then she wouldn't have to worry about facing him. By the time she saw him again he might have got over the ridiculous idea that she had been having an affair with Sam Rinde.

'Did you get the interviews you wanted, dear?'

Stephanie stifled a grin. 'Yes, Mum. You'll have to listen to the programme this morning. Which reminds me, I'd better get moving.'

She replaced the phone and picked up the tapes of her

interview with Sam Rinde. Her own programme could fit in a four-minute section which could serve to whet the appetite for the longer tracks, but to get the news comments would mean editing. Her studio time was booked and she began making exact timing for the comments she wanted. It took up every minute of her air time and she had to breathe deeply a few times to steady herself. She smiled at her announcer's introduction about coming down from the heights of the mountains as he welcomed her back. She switched on the microphone and began her comments, ad-libbing the introduction.

She was so intent on listening to the tape herself she was almost caught out for her following interview. She caught a 'well done' signal from the next studio and smiled in acknowledgment. The receptionist stopped her on her way from the studio at the end of the programme to tell her the boss wanted to see her. Stephanie walked along to the room, wondering if the accounts department were querying her expenses, but the warm congratulations of the station manager relieved her, and he agreed to a special segment to play the tapes in entirety.

Almost floating on air, Stephanie drifted through the rest of her preparations. In order to allow for trailers to promote the interview she selected a couple of witty comments from the tapes which had to be edited. They fitted together brilliantly. It seemed as though everything she touched simply turned out perfectly. By the time she greeted Mat after work her mood was one of elation.

'Stephanie, you clever girl—congratulations! I've just been listening. It sounded fun.'

'Mat, he was a great person to interview. I'm only just beginning to realise how lucky I was.'

'Luck, my foot! He had the good sense to realise that you were an interviewer he could trust,' snorted Mat. 'Goldie always said you were tops. Have you heard from him, by the way?'

'Yes, I rang him last night. He probably made a point of listening today.'

'I'll bet he did! Stephanie, you haven't heard our news. We've bought a house!'

'You have? In Timaru? What's it like?'

'We found it last weekend. It's wonderful. Of course, it's a little bit dearer than we hoped, but I guess that's always the way. We've studied our budget and decided we can afford it.'

'That's great news. How's the baby?'

'Growing rapidly! Come and see.'

Stephanie followed Mat and a moment later Ray arrived. Looking at her two friends with their infant, Stephanie could see the love between them. It made their company something to treasure.

'I've rung your mother to offer assistance, but she turned me down,' said Mat. 'Said I had enough to do with the baby and planning for the house. She's terrific!'

'Barbara has been helping her and I'll leave work early on Friday,' put in Stephanie as she played with the baby. 'You are just gorgeous!'

'Just like me,' laughed Ray.

'Hey, that's my line,' said Mat. 'Tell us all about the trip. I love Mount Cook, it's a great place for a honeymoon. Did you meet Dare?'

It was, felt Stephanie, unfortunate that her friend should have run the two comments together. Mount Cook with Dare would be reaching the stars. She banished the idea of the cloud being pierced between Dare and herself. He had been home long enough to dispel it, but between the two of them they had only succeeded in making more of a fog. Besides, there was the wonderful Barbara.

With Mat and Ray she couldn't be miserable for long and she explained the events of the weekend. As they laughed over her tale of turning the speaker on full blast in the middle of the night Stephanie began to see the funny side of it too.

'What did Dare say the next morning,' asked Mat, as her laughter subsided. 'Quite a lot, I imagine, about types who try to broadcast without a transmitter!'

The baby's demand for attention diverted the topic, much to Stephanie's relief. Final planning for the party and arranging transport took up the rest of the time as they had dinner and Stephanie left early, knowing that Mat had been up early with the baby. It suited her own need too, as she was feeling the effects of all the emotional hazards of the journey. As she drove home she wondered if Dare would deliberately stay away from the party. Oddly enough, she decided she did want him there even if he did glower at her all night. Mat had never met Dare, she reflected. She wondered what she would think of him. They would probably get on well together. Sourly she decided she was the odd one out. At least, she reminded herself, she had work to keep her busy. She admitted to herself that she was disappointed that Goldie hadn't rung her after hearing her success, but then she remembered the accounts war on toll calls. Goldie would probably send her a letter once he received copies of the tapes.

Work kept her busy until the last moment on Friday afternoon. She picked up the last-minute supplies from the caterer and with a feeling of relief drove out to the farm. Her mother had told her that Dare was still away. When she arrived at the farm her brother helped her unload the car.

'There's enough here for two parties!' he exclaimed. 'Mum and Barbara have been busy, but they obviously were not the only ones. That was a great interview,' he added. 'He sounded a real character.'

'He is. He was a bit reserved at the start, but we ended up friends. I hope to see him again before he leaves. But he'll be back, I know. As a matter of fact he could be in Christchurch one day.'

'Well, if he wants a look at a typical Kiwi farm, all sheep and no money, tell him he's welcome.'

'I'll do that,' promised Stephanie with a laugh. 'Careful with that box, it's precious.'

'What is it?' asked Alan.

'A gift for Ray and Mat. The rest of the social committee organised it while I was away, and the boss asked me to bring it out.'

'I'll put it in the front room, then.'

'We've got the barbecue all set. Just hope it doesn't pour,' he finished.

'Do be cheerful,' tossed Stephanie. She stopped and looked at her brother. 'What's the matter with you? You look as though you might be sickening for the mumps or something equally stupid.'

'Something equally stupid,' agreed Alan with a touch of his usual humour. 'This box of goodies to go in the deep-freeze?'

'Yes, please, Alan.'

Barbara seemed happy flitting about helping. Stephanie had to admit she was not only pretty, but capable, and she felt worse than ever. She viewed herself with disgust.

'Telephone for you, dear.'

Stephanie took the proffered receiver and spoke. A moment later she turned to her mother. 'It's our producer. Can I invite him out?'

'Of course, he'll be most welcome.'

Stephanie looked at her watch and told Sam she would be along in forty minutes. It would take her that time to get back into town to meet her guest. She would have to tell him about the party and if he wished she could return him to town before it started. She couldn't help hoping that he would decide to stay, her family would enjoy meeting him, but so would her friends.

Sam was waiting for her, and his stories of his adventures trying goldmining in Arrowtown kept her entertained. On hearing of the party he insisted on stopping to buy some bottles at a hotel on the way. They were just coming out when a familiar car went past. If Dare thought she had driven off with Sam Rinde at Mount Cook he would probably think she had spent the intervening time with him. From the glower on his face when he saw them it seemed like it.

Stephanie could have laughed if she had not felt so much like weeping. She forced herself to be pleasant to her guest, pointing out interesting items on the way. The journey soon passed and they rolled in through the familiar gates. Stephanie parked her car, noting that Dare had left room for her to reach the car port. She wondered why he had called on her parents first, then remembered that Barbara was helping her mother.

There was quite a welcoming committee to greet Sam

Rinde, but there was no sign of Dare and Barbara. Stephanie guessed they had seized the chance of some privacy for even a few moments.

Alan had been about to check the back paddock and he offered a ride to Sam Rinde. Stephanie waved them off, then rejoined her mother in the kitchen. A short time later she heard Dare's car start. Her feelings seemed to hit rock bottom as she pictured Barbara and Dare together.

'Now, what can I help with next?' Barbara's pleasant voice asked.

Stephanie almost dropped the tray she was holding, in surprise. What was happening with Barbara? Why hadn't Dare wanted her with him?

'Let me see, perhaps you could make a start on the eggs,' Mrs Fernley suggested. 'How's Dare?'

Barbara laughed. 'He's as grumpy as a dog who's nosed a beehive!'

CHAPTER TEN

The house seemed full of exciting aromas and a convivial atmosphere soon grew as more guests arrived. By teatime the massive barbecue had been lit. Stephanie's duties as hostess kept her busy, but didn't stop her from looking out for a tall, dark-haired figure. When everyone else had arrived and there was still no sign of Dare she wondered what Barbara was thinking. She didn't appear unduly upset, as Alan was looking after her. A frown crossed Stephanie's brow as she wondered if her brother had fallen in love with Barbara. Could that be the 'something stupid' he had mentioned? She sighed, certain that she had stumbled on the truth.

'Stephanie, come and join us,' Mat called insistently.

Stephanie assured herself that everyone looked happy, then went across to her friends. They were gathered round her father at the barbecue and Sam Rinde was doing his share of the entertaining. She was in mid-chuckle when she looked up and saw Dare.

'Stephanie, is that Dare?' whispered Mat with a quick gesture towards the distinctive figure greeting Mrs Fernley.

'That's Dare,' agreed Stephanie with a lightness she was far from feeling.

'I'm looking forward to meeting him,' said Mat.

Stephanie felt like saying that her feelings were exactly the opposite, but she refrained. Already her heartbeat felt less than steady, and all he had done was to walk up to her mother, then after a moment seek out Barbara. Stephanie was surprised how ragged she felt as she watched him smile at the other girl.

'I've just got to check the supper,' she said hastily as he turned in their direction. She fled to the kitchen and stayed there for a moment checking the stove, but everything was organised. Outside the barbecue food and salads were being handed round and she knew she would be needed during that period, so after taking a deep breath for courage she rejoined the party. The barbecue served to mix everyone up, and Stephanie joined in the laughter when a couple of lads went into the pool unprepared.

When Dare approached their group she slipped away to chat to some of the older staff members. She watched surreptitiously as he charmed Mat and Ray and felt indignant that they should so obviously get on well together. He seemed in no hurry to rejoin Barbara, a situation Stephanie found puzzling, until she realised that Barbara was helping her father and Alan serve the steaks, sausages and chops.

She collected up some of the empty plates, dishes and glasses. She carried them out to the kitchen, finding it a sanctuary.

'Hey, Stephanie, What are you doing hiding out here?' teased Ray, as he joined her a few minutes later.

'I'm not hiding,' she responded with a little too much alacrity. 'I just thought I'd put the dishwasher on and then the first load can be cleared.'

'Thought you were trying to avoid your ice man,' conceded Ray. 'We got on to the subject of rugby. Mat even did her famous replay of Canterbury's last try—had everyone laughing!'

Stephanie began beating some extra cream. It gave her something definite to do. Ray's lighthearted words had told her that at least Dare would know the truth. Hope and anguish mixed like flames burning in her thoughts. Since Dare's return he had constantly found her in situations which looked compromising. Even that day, he had seen Sam walk with her out of the hotel. He probably believed they had been together since Mount Cook.

'That cream's almost butter,' noted Ray. 'Leave it and come and dance with me. By the way, Sam Rinde is hitching a ride back to town with us. It will save you having to make the double trip.'

'That's great. But I'll say no to the dance, Ray, if you don't mind.' With her heart sore her feet would be like two lumps of lead.

'Well, just remember, Stephanie, Mat and I are there if you need us.'

Stephanie managed a watery smile as Ray left. She collected more dishes and cleared away the remains, then put the machine on again.

When she had finished she rejoined the party. Her eyes drifted over the crowd, seeking and finding Dare. He was in deep conversation with Barbara, and as he talked he was leading her towards the deserted pool area where the coloured lights set up a magical scene. Pain stabbed her. So much, she felt, for her hopes that Dare would at least say something about their earlier misunderstanding!

A couple of announcers called her to discuss a fine point and she joined them, reminding herself that Dare's attitude should make no difference. She had her career. Sam joined them and the discussion became hilarious. They were still laughing over one of his sallies when he turned to Stephanie.

'Let's go for a stroll round the pool,' he suggested.

He led the way with a slightly mystified Stephanie. She hoped they would not interrupt Dare and Barbara.

'Actually, I just wanted to get you on your own to tell you I've decided to go ahead with the film,' Sam told her. 'I decided just a little while ago.'

'Sam, that's wonderful news! Can I tell everyone?'

'No, don't do that. It's Ray and Mat's party and it's their night. They offered to take me back to town when they leave. I want to catch the first flight out in the morning. But I'll be back.'

'Sam, you terrible man! How can you tell me this without giving me a chance for an interview?' wailed Stephanie. Then inspiration hit her. 'Wait! The news team is here and there's always a recorder in their wagon. Please, Sam—I promise it won't take more than five minutes.'

Sam grinned. 'I might have guessed! I'll agree on condition you don't release it until after I've caught that overseas flight.'

Stephanie leaned forward and gave him a spontaneous kiss on the cheek. 'You are a darling!'

She ran to the car park, her mind already on the introduction and questions she would use. The familiar wagon was just in sight when a firm masculine hand on her shoulder brought her to a stop.

'Stephanie, I want to talk to you.'

She felt herself spun so that she was looking directly at the tall, dark-haired man.

'Let me go!' she snapped indignantly. Her temper rose as she imagined he had just left Barbara. How dare he stop her in such an authoritative way! she thought angrily.

'I found out some facts tonight and I just want to check something.'

Dare held her lightly and Stephanie felt herself pale under his regard. In the shadows of the trees along the drive she found his face full of angles and planes, disguising his expression. The old familiar tingle crept insidiously along her body as he pulled her towards him and she felt the warmth of his lean, hard body. She stiffened immediately, determining that she was not going to allow him to kiss her. Her breathing quickened as he ignored her instinctive withdrawal.

'I'm busy,' she squeaked, her voice ragged as Dare's fingers reached and stroked a spot at the base of her ear. She took a quick step back, knowing she had to break away.

'Just who do you think you are?' She spoke as firmly as she could, her wavering feelings tempered by resolution. 'You cast me in the role of butterfly, but I'm not flying into your net!'

Dare bent his head and sheltered her in the crook of his arm, stopping her flight. His mouth was almost level with her own and she knew a moment of pure panic.

'No, Dare!' she whispered, then melted in the exquisite sureness of his embrace, his lips firm and demanding. She felt her body respond as he kissed her, his voice softly whispering her name.

'Stephanie, darling butterfly.'

His mouth took hers again and she felt she was drowning in the feelings he had aroused. In the distance a car horn tooted sharply and broke the mood. She recalled in a flash her resolutions not to let Dare kiss her. Despair at her own weakness and Dare's attraction made her push him away.

'I said *no*, Dare!' she spoke fiercely, bolstering her own anger to help her defences. 'I'll put it more plainly, I don't want to ever see you again. I hate you!'

Incredibly she was free. Dare stood still as she steadied herself, then she turned and ran towards the wagon. Her heartbeats were racing and her mouth still had the taste of Dare's lips tingling on them. Almost automatically she climbed on to the seat. She sat still, her feelings exploding like firecrackers.

The strength of Dare's passion and the sweetness of his touch had shocked her. Her fingers trembled as she picked up the recorder. She didn't notice, her mind was still too full of the look of grey hurt on Dare's face at her outburst. She shivered, discovering she was cold, with icy trickles running over her body.

She had done the right thing, she told herself staunchly; Dare saw her only as a butterfly, not as a woman to be loved always and cherished as he loved and cherished Barbara. She felt pain rip through her.

'Dare, I love you,' she said slowly, wishing she had said those three words to him instead of telling him that she hated him. What, she wondered, would have happened? Bitterly she reminded herself that Dare had only one opinion of her.

It was too late! he was attracted to her, but it would never develop into love while he despised her for her relationships with every Tom, Dick and Harry. A so caught in her throat as she corrected herself. She should say Don, Ray and Sam—no doubt Dare did!

The tape recorder lay on her lap and she checked it mechanically. She was lucky, she had her work and in time she would forget Dare. The image of the totara tree growing tall and strong rose in her mind. There were, she reminded herself, plenty of other trees in the bush, and all had their share of attributes.

The bleep of the recorder made her realise that Sam Rinde would no doubt have given her up. She scrambled out and walked slowly towards the house. She saw Sam talking with another group, but he broke off as she approached.

'Let's try and keep the recorder hidden,' he said softly. 'Can we go into a room in the house?'

'Of course, I should have thought of that. We'll use my bedroom, it's at the far wing by the pool, so there should be no background noise.'

'By the way, I bought one of your friend's paintings,' he said. 'I wanted another he had on the wall, one of a golden butterfly woman. Quite incredible! I wasn't surprised when he said it wasn't for sale. Have you seen it?'

'Yes.' Stephanie bent hastily over the recorder. She wondered when Sam must have been to Dare's studio, then remembered Dare's late arrival. It was quite possible Barbara or Aunt Olivia had taken Sam over to the studio when she had been busy earlier.

'What did you think of it?' Sam persisted.

Stephanie spoke shortly. 'Not very much.'

Sam smiled. 'I was right—it was based on you. I wasn't one hundred per cent sure, but now I am. I thought he was attracted to you!'

'Nonsense,' protested Stephanie. Inside her she admitted Sam was right. There was an attraction as that kiss had proved yet again. But she didn't want a one-night stand, and Dare saw her only in that light.

'Let's get this interview done,' she pleaded, forestalling further questions by switching on the recorder. She did a quick check, then put her first question.

The interview was brief and succinct. Stephanie put a final question and Sam pondered a moment. Just as he was about to speak the door was thrust rudely open and Dare stood there, his face a mask of black anger. As he saw them and noticed the microphone and the tape recorder a look of incredulity swept over his face.

'You're interviewing Sam? Now?'

'That's right, Dare,' Stephanie spoke stiffly.

Sam broke in. 'Sit down, Dare. As I told you at Mount Cook, this girl of yours never stops working. I thought then no one would catch me being interviewed at one in the morning in my life yet, here I am again and it's almost two—an hour worse!'

'I'm sorry, I didn't realise.' Abruptly as he had arrived Dare departed.

Sam picked up the microphone from Stephanie's nerveless fingers and completed the final question without further prompting.

'Guess you'll be able to edit it later,' he smiled. 'Off you go and tell that man of yours you love him.'

Stephanie felt like crying at the gentleness of Sam tone, but she forced herself to pack up the gear.

'Thanks, Sam. I'll see you when you return.'

'You can count on that,' Sam promised. 'Looks like n chauffeur is here.'

'It's been a fantastic party, Stephanie,' greeted Mat. 'Ray and I will always remember it.'

Stephanie waved her friends off. As she turned she saw Barbara in Dare's arms. The kiss he gave her was just a fleeting brush, but it set up all sorts of stormy feelings in Stephanie. Anger began pounding in her as she recalled his eruption into her bedroom. She almost ran along to the porch where the head announcer was saying farewell to her parents. With the tape in her hand she thrust forward with a brief explanation, then remembered the recorder. She collected it from her bedroom and went to the familiar news wagon just as the team were leaving.

'Stephanie, I want to talk to you.' Dare's voice startled her.

'Well, I've no desire to talk to you, you arrogant, self-righteous prig!' Stephanie hissed, her temper exploding. 'I'm not going to talk to you, now or ever!'

'Oh, yes, you are.'

'This is ridiculous! I'm not lowering myself with an argument.' Stephanie wished she hadn't seen the ghost of a smile appear at Dare's mouth. She stalked towards the porch, her shoulders back, her head erect, trying to ignore Dare walking beside her.

A group called to her to say goodbye.

'You can see I'm busy,' she snapped. 'I have to look after my guests.'

Dare took her arm. The words bit. 'I'll see you at the otara tree at eleven o'clock. Be there,' he added threateningly, then turned and strode away towards his studio.

Gradually the last stragglers left. Stephanie didn't want to think about Dare's words. She couldn't afford to, she acknowledged. She most certainly would not be at the totara tree at eleven o'clock. The cheek of him, to order her to be there! She bristled angrily at the mere thought remembering the glimpse she had when he had kissed Barbara. Why, he was just a two-timing Don Juan, and he dared to lecture her!

Some of the social committee stayed behind to help her clear up. It was amazing how quickly the house was restored to order, and when they had left Stephanie wandered around the garden trying to find some comfort from the words which echoed and re-echoed in her brain.

'I'll see you at the totara tree at eleven. Be there!'

She sat down in an abandoned chair and looked up at the sky for some answer. The darkness seemed to be as empty of hope as she felt. Gradually in the east she saw a lightening, then a faint golden glow began appearing, folding and gathering back the grey, purple and black cloth of the night. The trees around the pool seemed like black etchings scratched against the gold. Inevitably she thought of Dare; she knew he would appreciate the scene.

With an effort she went to her room. Of course, she would not keep the appointment. She would go to bed and sleep the clock round—it would serve Dare Nayton right to be left cooling his heels at the totara tree! The thought gave her satisfaction and she curled up in bed with a smile.

It was striking nine when she woke and she shot out of bed in a hurry, trying to remember what was so important. Memory returned almost immediately and she hesitated. Of course she wasn't going to see Dare. She might as well go back to sleep. A steady hum in the background told her that her mother was busy vacuuming. Again she recalled the day she had been cleaning the flat and h mother's telephone call had announced Dare's return. That had been the end of her peaceful, calm existence.

'I'll feel better after a shower,' she told herself. 'Just morning blues!'

She washed her hair under the shower, letting the long thick strands form a brown collar. She clipped it carefully into position with the practice of years and pulled on her old jeans and an old sweater.

'See, I told you I wasn't going to meet Dare,' she lectured her reflection in the mirror.

Feeling a lot safer in her scruffy clothes, she went out to the kitchen.

'It was a grand party, darling,' Mrs Fernley greeted her. 'You left everything well organised.'

'Wasn't just me, Mum. Here, let me take that.'

'No, sit down and eat your breakfast. There's a stack of extra crockery to go back to your Aunt Olivia. You could take it back for me.'

Stephanie looked at the box. She didn't want to go anywhere near Dare Nayton.

'I'll put it in the car and give you the keys, Mum. Then you and Aunt Olivia can have a good old gossip about the party.'

'I think I'd like that,' her mother smiled. 'We're both quite certain there's going to be a lot of extra entertaining ahead.'

Stephanie felt her heart drop to the floor. Quite obviously her mother was in possession of a secret. Dare must have told her he was becoming engaged. Stephanie began to put a different construction on the meeting she had ordered. Some sense of chivalry he possessed must have told him that she would not like to hear the announcement of his engagement to Barbara in public.

The totara tree was simply the first place he had thought of where they could be guaranteed privacy. But why had he kissed her as he had, the evening before? Why had he been furious when he thought she was entertaining Sam Rinde in her bedroom? It didn't make sense.

A gust of wind blew a scattering of leaves from the scarlet oak in the corner of the garden. As she drank her tea Stephanie watched the light play on them as they drifted silently like bright butterflies. The thought made her cross again. Why had Dare painted her? If he loved Barbara, why didn't he make her the girl he loved to paint? Barbara was pretty, with her blonde hair and blue eyes.

'Alan's gone into town, dear, so there'll be no lunch to worry about,' said her mother. 'Your father took a snack with him, he's fixing some fencing at the boundary. I'll probably stay and have some lunch with Olivia. You just make something you feel like. The fridge is full of food.'

Absently, Stephanie waved her mother goodbye. It was ten-thirty. She heard the familiar whinny of her father's horse cropping in the paddock. She would go for a ride. That would make sure she was fully occupied at eleven o'clock.

She took off her old sweater and put on a fluffy green one, and a jacket, telling herself it would give her more protection on her ride. Within a remarkably short time she was cantering towards the back of the farm. She saw her father and waved to him, then turned back to the bush boundary. Her watch told her it was almost eleven.

Slowly she eased the chestnut into a walk as she approached the bush. She might as well see Dare as she just happened to be at the bush, she told herself. After all, she had to face the totara tree picnic spot sooner or later, and she might as well overlay that first tender memory with another. She could well find that the spot meant nothing at all.

Hooking the reins back so the horse could graze freely, she climbed over the fence into the bush. The scrubby bushes which marked the entrance scarcely seemed to have changed in the intervening years. Tiny-leaved manuka and kiokio ferns competed for footholds. Stephanie pushed aside a clinging vine of the native passion flower, its tiny tendril opening into a delicate flower. A cluster of pigeonwood trees made her smile wryly as she noted the differing male and female trees. At least, she thought, they could hardly run off to mother if they had a row! For a moment her step lightened as she had a mental image of a tree prancing along with its roots indignantly curled back.

The clearing was just ahead, and she felt a chill settle. If Dare was going to tell her about his engagement she must congratulate him with a smile. She would not allow him to guess her foolish dreams—dreams she hadn't even allowed herself. The bush was silent apart from the chirpy whistle of a few wax-eyes flitting about. Instinctively she checked her watch. It was one minute to eleven.

Sunlight filtered through the differing shades of green. Above her the totara reached skywards, its growth majestic. Automatically Stephanie crossed the open space to the foot of the tree and gazed around her. No one was there. She had nothing to fear. It was just an old picnic spot.

'I've been stupid,' she announced in a clear tone. 'Abysmally, totally stupid.'

'That makes two of us, then,' came the unexpected answer.

She looked round. Dare came from behind the tree, his eyes holding hers. Stephanie felt her heartbeat increased just to look at him. With insight she realised it wasn't the scene she had to stay away from, it was the person. Somewhere a bird shrieked in alarm, and she wished she could flee just as easily.

'Thank you for coming,' Dare said politely.

'I was down this way,' she muttered ungraciously. She wished Dare didn't have that wretched habit of almost laughing at times. It was just the way he curved his lips. She found her eyes on them and was surprised at the degree of feeling that coursed through her. It was better to get the scene over quickly, she felt.

'I presume you want to tell me you're getting engaged to Barbara Wade,' she managed. 'Congratulations.'

Dare looked at her in some surprise. Had he imagined she would burst in tears? she thought angrily. He was right, of course, but she would make sure he never knew.

'No, I wanted to apologise to you, Stephanie. This seemed the right place. You're right, Barbara is getting engaged.' He paused, and Stephanie clenched her fingers inside her jacket to hide her feelings. 'But not to me. She's in love with Alan.'

'To Alan?' Surprise made Stephanie's eyes widen. Joy and hope bubbled through her. 'Oh, I'm so glad!'

Instantly contrite, she slapped her hand over her mouth. 'Dare, I'm sorry. I spoke without thinking.' Tentatively she touched his arm in apology. She spoke softly careful of his feelings. 'She's a lovely girl.'

'You're right, Stephanie, Barbara is a very special person.'

Stephanie felt the tiny bubble inside her burst and disappear. Dare continued to gaze at her, but she could not read his eyes. They were sombre and sad.

'Is that why you came home—to marry?' she asked quietly.

'I'm not sure. Possibly meeting Barbara made me think about someone else.'

Stephanie felt her heart fluttering like a frightened bird.

'I don't understand,' she managed.

Dare took her hand and studied each finger as though he would memorise them. His touch and his nearness made her feel breathless, but she was determined he would not know the effect he had on her.

'I had to find out how I felt about you, Stephanie.'

'Me?' Thoughts raced in a mad scurry through her mind scattering when Dare traced the heart line on her palm. Quickly she pulled her hand away. 'You despised me,' she whispered, discovering her voice had disappeared.

'I wanted to hate you, but I couldn't. I thought you'd broken every code I'd ever respected. You made me jealous and angry. You looked so fragile and so innocent, yet I was sure you were completely heartless. I'd loved you yet you had tossed me over without even a word. At least that's what I thought.'

The totara above them held them absorbed in the quietness of the moment. Dare moved again and his eyes held a yearning that tugged at her heart.

'I'm sorry, Stephanie. I've made you hate me because I couldn't and wouldn't trust you. When I met Mat last night everything slotted into place. I remembered that I'd been wrong over young Romeo and I began to wonder if I'd been wrong over the other men. I'd seen you at Mount Cook with Sam Rinde, yet from his comments about Queenstown I found out he hadn't spent the intervening time with you. Then he said something which made me realise his identity and I guessed that he was the reason you'd gone to Mount Cook.'

Dare picked up a stray leaf and held it gently between his fingers, as though reluctant to continue.

'Then I saw him go into your bedroom.' He looked at her, again the self-mocking smile cornered his lips. 'You were there—you must have guessed how I felt. Sam's comments about the recording told me the answer to the time I waited for you at the motel. But it was too late. You'd already turned against me. When I tried to explain you made your feelings perfectly clear.'

'But you kissed Barbara,' put in Stephanie dazedly.

'Not the way I kissed you. I guess I always liked her and we shared several interests. She'd just told me about Alan. When I was at Mount Cook I hoped Alan and Barbara would have a chance to get to know each other better.

'Whenever I saw you I felt totally different and I assure you very primitive emotions. The whole truth is that I never stopped loving you.'

Silence drifted between them. Stephanie was still trying to believe Dare's words.

'I can't excuse what I did to you, Stephanie,' he went on. 'Jealousy is a bad emotion. I can't blame you in any way. I know it's too late to repair our relationship.'

He held her swiftly and dropped a brief butterfly kiss on her lips.

'That's for goodbye, my darling.'

The bubble that had been bursting with hope in her heart exploded at his touch. When he released her Stephanie threw her arms around him. He looked so stern and fierce that for a moment she was surprised at her own bravery.

'I love you, Dare.' She whispered the words into the broad chest, finding that much easier than looking at him.

He stiffened. 'What did you say?'

Stephanie felt her face gently held so that he could read the love in her eyes. 'I love you, Dare,' she repeated softly.

It was like a miracle seeing the joy dazzle from his eyes. Instantly she was held firmly in his arms, his mouth crushing hers, seeking, demanding and finding. She felt herself responding to the magic of his touch, passions aflame with joy and wonder.

Dare kissed her again and again, covering her with kisses, his voice whispering endearments in her ear. When he stopped for a moment just to look at her she met his gaze almost shyly.

'Terrific!' he whispered. 'My little golden butterfly!'

But this time there was nothing two-edged about the words. Surrounded by Dare's love, Stephanie knew the words would hurt no longer. She smiled mistily at him, her fingers entwined into the thick dark curls.

'I said I'd love you for ever, my darling.' Dare kissed her lightly and tenderly, his blue eyes gleaming in their brightness. He spoke softly. 'And I'll love you for ever and a day.'

A WORD ABOUT THE AUTHOR

Rosalie Henaghan began her first book shortly after she interviewed fellow New Zealander and Harlequin Romance author Essie Summers on a radio program. "I've often thought I could write a book," Rosalie innocently commented, and in her kindly way, Essie urged her to try.

Now the author of many books, Rosalie is an expert at making use of events and elements of her own life to enhance her stories. One of her heroines is a teacher—as she herself was trained to be. Broadcasting forms a background for another novel, reflecting Rosalie's former profession as a radio personality.

Sometimes, says the author, her heroines are more capable than their creator! Though Rosalie would love to be an adept knitter, for instance, at least one of her heroines is far better at that activity than Rosalie could ever hope to be. Or, she might send a character in a story out into the garden to weed when her own garden is a mess!

Rosalie believes in observing carefully what is close at hand. She is convinced that a writer should examine his or her own backyard, and then, she says, "as Essie told me—start writing."

THE GOLDEN CAGE

The first Harlequin American Romance Premier Edition by bestselling author ANDREA DAVIDSON

Harlequin American Romance Premier Editions is an exciting new program of longer–384 pages!–romances. By our most popular Harlequin American Romance authors, these contemporary love stories have superb plots and true-to-life characters–trademarks of Harlequin American Romance.

The Golden Cage, set in modern-day Chicago, is the exciting and passionate romance about the very real dilemma of true love versus materialism, a beautifully written story that vividly portrays the contrast between the life-styles of the run-down West Side and the elegant North Shore.